Doctor Frost

S.L. Sterling

DOCTOR FROST

by

S.L. STERLING

© 2024

Doctor Frost

Copyright © 2024 by S.L. Sterling

ISBN: 978-1-989566-87-9

Paperback ISBN: 978-1-989566-98-5

Editor: Brandi Aquino, Editing Done Write

Cover Design: Thunderstruck Cover Design

Doctor Frost

His name suits him well and he hates Christmas. Bottom line, Doctor Frost is a grumpy jerk.

I'm sure he has his reasons. We all do. Yet I won't be his punching bag in what you could call a rather combative relationship.

The day his daughter shows up crying I take pity on him and step in to offer some womanly advice. That's when I find out the reason for his horrible demeanor, and my heart goes out to him.

I didn't expect that information to change things. Soon I find myself looking at him a little differently. We start talking, and I start getting to know his kids, and soon I'm doing more than just dreaming of tasting his lips.

Just as things begin to take a turn, a rival nurse has other plans. She is willing to do whatever it takes to keep us apart.
Only she doesn't know who she is up against. I'm feisty and Doctor Frost is grumpy and together we will fight for what we both want this Christmas.

Dalton

NOVEMBER

Rain hit my office window, the steady tap annoying me, pulling my focus away from the report I was working on. It had been a long day and combined with the steady giggling from the girls out at the front desk, I was growing more annoyed by the minute. What did they think this was, a playground?

I let out a sigh, flipped to the next screen, and went to write more of my report when I got to one section of my notes and couldn't read them. I frowned as I stared at the messy handwriting. I'd asked my nurses to add this part when I was on my way out of an appointment. They should have better penmanship than this. My writing was one thing, but this was inexcusable.

When another round of laughter erupted through my

wall, I got up from behind the desk and took off out my door and around to the front desk.

Charlotte took half a glance in my direction, stopped laughing, and focused on whatever it was she was supposed to be working on, but when I set my sights on Amelia, she sat there looking up at me with a huge grin on her face.

It was always the same with her, and it had been that way since she'd started working for me. She was always certain that people could be cured. It was exhausting when I knew that wasn't the case. I looked at Charlotte and then over to that grin again.

"Last I checked, it's only two. There are three more hours before you're finished today, which means you should do the work that needs to be done and not be goofing off. This office should be silent," I said, slamming the patient file I had questions about down on the counter in front of Amelia.

Charlotte jumped, but Amelia sat there giving me that look. She cleared her throat, rested her chin on her hand, and met my eyes.

"We are just creating a healthy work environment," she bit back. "Everyone knows laughter is good for the soul. Something you should do a little more of."

My jaw clenched as I placed my hand on the desktop and opened the file I'd brought out. Then I met her eyes. "Are you saying this isn't a healthy work environment?"

She'd been a thorn in my side ever since she'd started working for me. She was always cheerful, always bubbly, something that any doctor in this hospital would probably love to have. She was also attractive and beautiful as hell, but she was also always talking back and put a lot of effort into making my life hell. It was exhausting and, as of late, had been irritating me more than ever.

"Is there something you needed? If not, I'd like to go back to laughing and having fun while we finish out our day." She rested her chin on her hand, giving me that adorable grin I absolutely hated.

I shoved the file at her as I stared down into those big cinnamon eyes. "Page three...halfway down there is some sort of scribble. Can you tell me what you wrote there?" I questioned, remembering that it was her working with me that day.

She smiled at me, slowly taking the file while looking me directly in the eyes. "Sure thing, Doctor Frost!"

She opened the file, flipped to the third page, and ran her finger down the page, stopping at the scribble mark. She studied it for a moment as I watched her, then frowned and swallowed hard before looking back at me. Did she not know what it said, either?

"Well?" I grunted.

"This mark here?" she asked.

"Yes, Amelia, that mark right there."

"Geez, I'd love to help you out, but I don't have a clue

what it is. Besides, that is your handwriting," she said, pressing her lips together as she closed the file and placed it back on the counter in front of me.

I looked at her, at those beautiful cinnamon eyes, growing more irritated by the second as she looked up at me while the phone rang. Charlotte quickly grabbed it, whispering as I locked eyes with Amelia.

"And you know, you really ought to say please when you ask someone to help you with something. Just adds, oh...I don't know, a touch of something to the question." She shrugged.

I felt as if my head were going to explode. She'd been on me about that recently whenever I'd given her direct orders on anything. She reminded me every single time, just like now, that I should say please and thank you.

"Amelia..." I barked, only to be stopped by Charlotte quietly clearing her throat.

"Doctor Frost?" she said, her voice squeaking.

I turned my attention toward her, waiting for her to speak.

"What?" I barked when she didn't immediately start talking.

"One of your patients would like to see you..." she said, her voice cracking. "She's up on floor fifteen, room 223."

I glanced at my watch and then let out a sigh. I'd already done my rounds for today. I'd had all the patient interaction I'd wanted. I was about to tell her to put it off until tomorrow when I saw Amelia looking at me.

"Fine. Pull the file, Amelia. Let's go."

Only she didn't move. She just sat there, giving me that same smug smile she'd given me for the past few minutes.

"NOW!" I barked, causing her to jump for the first time. Poor Charlotte almost dropped the phone and had to take a drink before she answered the line and let them know we were on our way.

I didn't wait for another word. I took off out of my office and made my way toward the elevator, quickly pressing the call button, hoping I could get up there before she arrived, but just as the doors opened, Amelia appeared at my side. We both loaded into the elevator and stood in silence as we waited to get to the fifteenth floor.

We made our way to the unit the patient was in, and I quickly exchanged information with the doctors and nurses on duty before I decided if I actually needed to see the patient or just change her treatment plan. At least they'd called me to get my opinion before doing anything. Once I'd gotten the information I needed, I made my decision and looked over at Amelia, who waited patiently by my side, pen at the ready to make any notes.

"Go tell Mrs. Jackson I'm switching her off the medication that is making her sick to a new one," I muttered, while writing down the name of the new medication in the chart for the nurses.

When I handed the clipboard back to the nurse and turned toward Amelia, she was staring at me.

"What is it?" I questioned.

"Does that mean you aren't going to come in and talk to her?" she questioned. "She specifically asked to see you. She probably has questions."

I averted my eyes. I swore if she started, I was going to explode. I let out the breath I was holding and then looked back at her and nodded over to the right. I took a few steps and waited until she made her way over to me.

"Amelia, there is no need for me to go in and speak with her. You can take care of this."

"Doctor Frost, that woman has been your patient since she got sick. You really should—"

"Amelia, worry about yourself and what I just told you to do. Now, go and speak with her."

"Seriously? She's dying, Dalton." Amelia frowned, looking up at me.

As I studied her, I noticed her eyes getting watery. "I know, it's you that normally doesn't acknowledge that."

Amelia looked at me. I was certain I saw a hint of a tear in her eyes, but she swallowed hard and straightened her back. "Dalton..."

"Amelia, don't make the patient wait any longer. I have to go. I have work to do and test results to go over. I need to prepare for the day tomorrow, and so do you. It's best you take care of this patient now, rather than later." Without waiting for her to respond, I turned and went to take a step when I heard Amelia clear her throat.

"I can't believe you! Are you serious? You really won't speak with her?"

I looked over my shoulder at her, at the disappointment and anger on her face. "Yes, Amelia, believe it," I said, taking another couple of steps away from her.

"What about please? What if I ask you to please speak with her?" she begged.

I didn't have time for games. Ignoring her, I made my way to the elevator where I hit the call button and waited. While I waited, I glanced over my shoulder to see if she'd done what I'd asked. Instead, I saw her wipe at her eyes and then glare at me.

The elevator doors opened, and I stepped inside, turning to see her still standing there, the look in her eyes now one of disappointment. I didn't care, though; I hit the button for my fifth-floor office and watched as the doors closed.

IT WAS a little after seven when I shut the light off in my office and pulled the door closed. The office was dark aside from the small overhead lights at the check-in counter, which normally stayed on until the last person left, which was normally me.

I reached to turn them off when I heard something hit the floor. I glanced around the corner to see Amelia bent down on one knee, picking up a stack of files, stacking them once again into a neat pile.

"What are you still doing here?"

She jumped and dropped the stacked files off her knee as she looked over her shoulder at me.

"Oh my god, you scared me. I thought you left hours ago," she muttered, picking up the files and stacking them again.

"You didn't answer me," I barked.

She didn't say anything as I waited, and then she let out a sigh.

"You didn't answer me either. If you need to know, I'm here because Mrs. Jackson had questions and concerns, so I stayed with her for over an hour and a half, doing my best to answer them. I then had to finish up my work for today and prep for tomorrow, which was what I was doing until you made me drop the patient files."

Why had she been with the patient that long when all she needed to do was give her a simple answer?

"What questions did she have?"

Amelia huffed and looked over toward me as she stood up. "If you wanted to know, you should have gone to see her," she barked.

"Well, if you needed help, you should have called me."

Ignoring me, she grabbed the rest of the files and put them in a messy pile as she muttered something under her breath.

"What was that?" I questioned, my voice taking on a stern tone.

She let out a sigh and shook her head.

"What did you say, Amelia?"

She stood up and turned toward me. "I said, lots of good that would do. You couldn't even take five minutes to come in and see her, as if I was going to call you."

"Amelia, you've worked with me for what, a year? You should know I don't hold the hands of my patients. Now, if they have a concern, of course, it's my job to answer them, but..."

"That's just it. It is your job, not mine. You should have been there to listen to her. Instead, you couldn't or wouldn't. I'm not sure which it was because you claimed you had work to do. So, why on earth would I call you and bother you? I took the time, answering questions I'm not even sure I gave the correct answers to, even though I had work to do as well, which is why I am still here."

"Amelia, that's enough. I don't like your tone."

"You know, last I checked, you are a doctor, and you are supposed to have some sort of bedside manner. Instead, all I've seen is a cold-hearted man who treats patients as objects instead of showing compassion to the emotional, scared people they become when they are ill. It's disgusting."

If ever I'd felt irritated, it was now, right at this moment. She'd overstepped. I had a fucking heart, and I showed compassion, and I had a fucking great bedside manner. All she needed to do was look at the awards I'd gotten in the last year. I was about to speak, but she held out her hand, stopping me.

"Dalton, I don't want to hear it. All you do is stomp around, yell out orders as if we are some sort of waitstaff instead of colleagues. We can't laugh, we can't have fun. You know the other day Mrs. Linton even commented how different this office had become, and she'd only been in here to pick up her prescription. I don't know who the hell ever pissed you off that bad, to make you into this sort of person. Life in this office is a living hell sometimes, but I can't imagine what home must be like for you. Honestly, I feel sorry for your significant other, if this is what she has to deal with day in and day out."

Amelia, red-faced and out of breath slammed the stack of files down on the desk. She bent over, grabbed her purse from the drawer, and then went for her coat, but the phone rang. Not thinking, she grabbed the receiver and in an almost unrecognizable voice from the last few moments sang, "Hello..."

She didn't look at me. Instead, she shoved the phone out in front of her.

"We don't answer calls after the office is closed. Now, take a message and I'll call them back in the morning," I barked.

"It's your daughter. Do you want to take it, or would you like me to tell her what a grump you are?" she questioned, looking me directly in the eye.

I was seething with anger as I ripped the phone from her hand. "Hello."

"Dad...sorry to call you at work. Mrs. Jenkins wanted to know what to prepare for supper tonight. You left nothing on the sheet."

I looked up to see Amelia staring at me with hateful eyes. I'd definitely have to deal with her, but right now, I needed to get home to the kids. Her words, which were way out of line, had struck a chord, one I didn't even remember having. Had I really become that bad?

Okay, perhaps I'd grown a little cold here at work, but she had no right to attack my personal life the way she had. That was far over the bounds of a professional relationship.

"Tell Mrs. Jenkins I'll be bringing home dinner. I should be there in...oh, thirty minutes," I said, glancing at my watch and then back at Amelia. "See you soon," I said, and then held the receiver out in front of me for Amelia to take.

She hesitantly grabbed the receiver from my hand, hanging it up. I was going to say something to her, reprimand her for answering the phone, but decided against it. Instead, I turned and made my way to my office and stopped at the door. I didn't need to look back, I knew she was staring at me. I could feel her eyes boring into the back of my head.

"Oh, Amelia. Take tomorrow off. I'll see you back here on Wednesday. Then I will figure out what the punishment shall be for talking back to your boss."

I didn't give her time to respond; I pushed the door open and walked out of the office, doing my best to calm down before heading home to my kids.

Amelia

I SAT inside The Cooling Rack, waiting for Charlotte to meet me after her shift. It was probably a good thing he'd forced me to take the day off today, to give me time to cool down. If only it had worked. I was still angry over everything that had happened yesterday but was now starting to feel sick.

To top it off, I woke up with a horrible headache, teetering on the edge of a migraine and probably would have either called in or went home sick anyway. Or it could have ended up way worse. Perhaps, I would have told him off again and would have found myself jobless, or maybe he'd already decided my fate, and I didn't know I was jobless. I already knew that option wasn't off the table. I'd been pretty horrible to him, and even though I regretted some of the things I'd said, I knew in my mind he'd deserved it.

I'd worked for Doctor Frost, or Dalton as most co-workers referred to him, for almost a year, and he'd been an asshole since day one. I'd hoped that over time there would have been something, some sort of gentler, softer side to him, but there was nothing. He was nothing but short, snippy, and rude to everyone who crossed his path, but it seemed he was worse with me. I swore the only reason he kept his job was because his patients loved him. Even when I'd sat with Mrs. Jackson, she couldn't say a bad thing about him, which blew my mind.

Staff differed from patients. They all had the same feelings toward him I did. At least that was what they told me. I'd brought him up to Connie, the head RN in the hospital. She worked in the emergency department and there had been a couple of times I'd helped out there after a run-in with him. She'd listen and sympathize but then would be different to him in person.

It always blew my mind how no one stood up to him, either. He'd bark orders at them, and they would just do as they were told. Only when it came to me, he was way worse. I would not cower from him like the rest of them, which was why I'd blown up at him. It honestly hadn't surprised me I'd finally lost control over myself when he wouldn't come and speak with that sweet woman who spent over an hour crying on my shoulder. In my mind, it wouldn't hurt the man to show some sort of compassion once in a while.

"My god, what did you do?" Charlotte whispered under her breath as she slid into the seat across from me.

"What? Why?" I questioned, wondering if maybe he had changed overnight and became human.

She blew out the breath she was holding and looked over at me. "That man was more than unbearable today. If you think he's cranky on a normal day..." She looked up at me, her eyes wide. "He was hellish today. So, whatever you said to him last night pissed him off."

I looked down at the menu in front of me, still trying to decide what it was I wanted to order as I thought about everything I'd said to him last night. Thank God Charlotte hadn't been there to witness it.

"I stood up to him. It wasn't anything that didn't need to be said, except, well, except for the fact I may have overstepped with my words when it came to his personal life. But, honestly, Charlotte, the man deserved it."

"You what? You mean you actually talked back to Doctor Frost? Like while you were working, and you brought his personal life into it?" she questioned, her eyes widening with disbelief.

I nodded.

"What did he say?"

"He said nothing. The man was actually speechless for

once, and you should have seen the look on his face. It was like he didn't care at all about what I was saying."

"I bet he did."

"I'm telling you, it fell on deaf ears."

"Maybe at the moment, but not afterward. I think whatever you said stirred something inside of him. I've never seen him act the way he did today. He was worse than ever. He even lost it with Sawyer and Connie."

Here I'd hoped what I said would have struck a chord and turned him into the opposite of what he was. Instead, from the sounds of it, I'd made it worse.

"I probably should have kept my mouth shut, but honestly, when he wouldn't go see Mrs. Jackson, I guess that was my breaking point. Honestly, that wasn't really the last straw, it was the fact that she had nothing bad to say about him at all. She sat there thanking him for changing the one medication, praising him for being an amazing doctor. The woman is dying, she was upset and scared and had a pile of questions. Her doctor refused to see her, and here she is upset as hell, of course, thanking a man who couldn't care less. It just pissed me off."

Charlotte nodded in understanding. Then looked up at me. "Are you afraid of facing him tomorrow?"

I shook my head. What was there to be afraid of? He's a grumpy, uncaring asshole. I only called it like it was.

"No. I'm sure he'll be his usual charming self toward me tomorrow, like always."

I could see all the questions lining her eyes, maybe even a hint of worry. She looked at me and bit her bottom lip.

"What is it?"

She let out a sigh. "Aren't you afraid he may fire you?"

I thought for a moment and then shook my head. "No, I think if he were going to do that, he would have done it last night after I told him I questioned how his significant other could stand to be around him."

"Amelia, you didn't." Charlotte looked at me with horrified eyes.

"Damn right I did. Like I said, I lost it. I couldn't take his lack of caring any longer." I shrugged, just as my cell phone vibrated against the table. I glanced down to see an email from Doctor Frost requesting my presence at a meeting tomorrow. I shoved my phone over to Charlotte and showed her the email. She bit her bottom lip as she read the message and then looked up at me, concern flooding her face.

"Well, all I can say is good luck with that tomorrow."

I'D SHOWN up to work early because of the meeting. Instead of finding Dalton in his office, it was empty. I figured he was running late, and instead of dwelling on it,

I went about my morning calling his patients to schedule their upcoming appointments.

Dalton still hadn't arrived by ten thirty, which I thought was odd, but again I wasn't going to worry about it. Instead, I grabbed my things and was about to head down on my break when the phone rang. It was Sawyer, one of the head ER doctors, requesting my help in the emergency room, which I happily volunteered for. If it meant getting out of this meeting with Mr. Grumpy, I was in.

I stopped and grabbed a coffee and bagel and then made my way over to the emergency room. The ER was crazy and looked like a bomb had gone off inside, which wasn't out of the ordinary. I placed my things behind the nurses' station, and that was when I saw Dalton. He was dealing with a patient over in the corner.

I sat down and took a bite of my bagel, waiting for Connie to give me some instruction. Not only was Connie my direct boss, but she was also Eastport General's gossip queen.

"Thanks for coming down. It must be nice to be recognized around here," she said, smiling as she sat down beside me.

"What do you mean?" I questioned.

"Well, I shouldn't tell you, but Dalton requested you."

"What?" I frowned.

She was about to say something when another ambulance pulled up to the bay doors just as Dalton appeared with some files, which he put on the desk. He looked at me as the EMTs brought a man in on a stretcher.

"Stabbing..." the one EMT mumbled to Dalton as they took him over toward an empty room.

"Amelia, looks like it's you and me. Let's go," he muttered.

Those are the nicest words the man has ever said to me, I thought to myself as I looked over at Connie, wondering what she'd meant, when I heard Dalton clear his throat.

"Coming."

I got up from my chair as two other nurses came rushing over to help us. It was touch-and-go for a while. The patient had lost a lot of blood, but we finally got him stabilized. Once our job was done, I stepped out of the room, closing the curtain and pulling my gloves off, dumping them into the trash while the other two nurses worked on finishing up the stitches.

I took my blood-covered gown off and dumped it into the laundry and then made my way over to the sink and began washing my hands when I heard someone clear their throat behind me. Glancing over my shoulder, I saw Sawyer standing there.

"Sorry, I'll be just a moment," I said, rinsing the soap from my hands.

"Amelia, you can head down on your break now. Janice just got in," Sawyer said, coming up beside me and shoving his hands under the warm water.

"Thanks." I smiled. "What a day. I'm beat, and I still have another, what, four hours?" I giggled.

"All part of the job. Keeps us young." He chuckled. "Brielle said you came into The Cooling Rack yesterday. She said it was nice to see you."

"Yeah, I had coffee with Charlotte. I was hoping she'd have Emma, but no luck. She doing well?"

"Yeah, she's getting so big. We'll have to have you over for dinner soon."

"I'd love that! Well, I guess I'll see you in an hour." I smiled and made my way down the hall toward the exit doors.

"Thanks for coming down last second. We appreciate it."

"No problem." I waved. "Glad I could help. It feels great to save lives."

I was just about to push the doors open to exit the emergency area when I heard my name called. Figuring it was Sawyer again, I stopped and turned, only to see Dalton following me.

"Wait up a moment," he said again.

Unsure what to expect, I just stood there waiting until he caught up with me. He'd missed our meeting, so he couldn't be pissed with me. He never thanked me for helping, which would have been nice after that last patient, but he said nothing. He just looked at me.

"Aren't you going to say anything? Thank me for an outstanding job?" I questioned, probably pushing my luck.

His eyes locked with mine. He just glared. Then he pushed the door open and took off in front of me.

"Yeah, you're welcome!" I shouted after him.

I stood there wishing that the things I'd said to him the other night would have resonated with him, but they apparently hadn't. Charlotte was right, he had become worse. At least, before he'd tell me I had to do a better job.

I was just about to push the doors open when Connie came out of the supply room with a handful of stuff.

"Connie, what did you mean earlier, that it must be nice to be recognized?" I questioned.

Connie stopped and smiled. "Well, by Dalton, of course."

"Huh?"

"He was the one who told Sawyer to call you. Said he wanted to work with one of the best nurses in the hospital. I just thought it must be nice to be thought of that way. I'll have to put that in your file."

I could have fainted right on the spot. Dalton had spoken about me that way? There was no way in hell he actually said those words after the way I'd spoken to him.

"What's your secret? It would be nice if some of the

other nurses were looked upon that way with the other doctors."

I swallowed hard and smiled, trying to come up with something other than to tell your boss off because that was what I'd done, and it had somehow earned me respect. It wasn't an appropriate answer to tell your direct boss though.

I swallowed hard. "Ah, just tell them to be a good team player. It took a long while to get noticed," I said, smiling. "I'm gonna grab some food. See you soon." I needed to get out of there before I did faint.

Dalton

"Dalton, welcome home," Mrs. Jenkins said as I walked through the door. Christmas music played, and the smell of dinner caused my stomach to grumble.

She began shoving the kids' shoes into the closet, then made her way into the living room tidying up where Tommy had clearly been playing with some toys after school.

"Good evening, Betty. How are you and the kids?" I questioned, hanging my coat in the closet, then taking off my shoes.

"Oh, I'm good and, of course, they're fine. Claire is doing her homework in the kitchen, and Tommy is upstairs working on his project. Neither of them wanted to eat their vegetables tonight. Apparently, Tommy no longer likes carrots and Claire no longer wants to eat corn, but that is how it goes."

Mrs. Jenkins had worked for us since Claire was born. When Kenzie passed, she stepped up and began working for us full time, helping me raise the kids and allowing me to continue my practice. She was part of the family.

I smiled. "That figures, last week, that was all they wanted." I chuckled as I placed my laptop bag down on the floor inside the doorway.

"How was your day at the hospital?"

"Hectic. Sorry I couldn't make it back in time for dinner, which smells delicious, by the way." I glanced at my watch, cringing. "Again, I'm sorry. I know you like to be home with your son by now."

"Dalton, it's nothing to worry about. After all these years, I know things get out of control at the hospital."

She continued to run around, picking up the toys Tommy had left, and then was about to head on down the hall toward the kitchen when I stopped her.

"Betty, you've done enough for today," I said.

"Nonsense. I was just going to plate your dinner, throw in a load of laundry, and do the dishes. Then I'll be on my way."

"No. I've kept you long enough today. You head on home. I can take care of those things. Plus, I know your son isn't here all the time and that you want to spend some time with your own grandkids."

"I know, but you and your children need me, too."

"I know. In all seriousness, you go. I'll drop the kids off at school in the morning and we will see you tomorrow night." I smiled.

"You're sure?" she asked, looking around at the mess that was still left to clean up. "There is still a lot to do."

"I'm positive." I smiled.

I waited at the door and helped her with her coat and then wished her a good night. Once I knew she was in her car and had backed out of the driveway, I made my way down to the kitchen, where I found Claire sitting at the table, agonizing over her homework.

"Hey there, sweetheart. How was school?" I questioned, plating up my dinner from the leftovers in the pan on the stove, popping it into the microwave to reheat it.

"Fine," she muttered.

"Only fine?" I chuckled.

I watched as she stared at her notebook, chewing on the end of her pencil like she was working on the hardest question in the world.

"What is it?" I questioned, just as the microwave beeped. "Do you need some help?"

"Oh no, I'm okay," she said, still staring at the paper in front of her.

"Okay then."

I grabbed my plate and carried it over to the table

where I sat down and cut into chicken and popped a piece into my mouth.

"Dad...can I ask you something?"

"Of course. Anything."

As she smiled up at me, all I could see was my wife. God, she looked just like Kenzie, and the older she got, the more the resemblance stood out. She had her hair and her eyes, even her smile was the same. Some days, it was hard to look at her without remembering everything about my wife, not that she was ever far from my mind.

"Well...there is this dance at school..."

"Ah, yes, I saw that permission form on the fridge door. The Christmas dance, right?" I questioned.

"Yes, you said I could go."

"Yes, and I signed the form. You took it into school, right? Or do I need to talk to your teacher?"

She nodded. "No, I took it in."

"Good." I turned my attention back to my plate. "So, what is this question you want to ask me?"

"Dad, I was wondering, would it be okay if I got my hair done for that? I've been saving my allowance, but I am short," she asked, looking up at me with hope in her eyes.

I looked at her, at her beautiful brown hair that had natural copper highlights, exactly like her mother, and cleared my throat.

"What did you want to do to your hair?"

She looked up at me and shrugged. "I just wanted to get it cut a little."

Relief flooded me. I was hoping she didn't want to colour it like some girls in her grade. Her hair was far too beautiful to change, and I'd have had a hard time agreeing to that.

"I think that could be done, and you keep your allowance." I winked.

"Thanks, Dad." Clair smiled and went back to her homework just as Tommy came into the kitchen, pulling the juice carton from the fridge with his small hands.

"What you doing there, sport?" I asked, watching him struggle to reach the table.

"I want some juice." He shrugged before making his way over to the cupboard to grab his cup off the counter.

He placed the cup down and was about to open the carton of juice, only I stopped him and did it for him, pouring him half a glass, then placing his glass in front of the empty chair.

"Thanks, Dad."

He sat down on the chair beside me while I continued to eat my dinner and Clair worked on her homework. I smiled as both my kids sat with me. We'd all gone through a hard change after losing Kenzie. She was taken so suddenly, and it had changed all of us. We'd all struggled to find a new dynamic, making our smaller family life work. It was hard, stressful, and I worried how not having a other might affect Clair and Tommy in the future. I did my best to be there for both of them, but I barely understood my own feelings.

"How would you guys like to hit the Christmas market on the weekend with Mrs. Jenkins?" I questioned.

Claire's eyes lit up. The Christmas market was something she'd always done with her mother and since she'd passed, I'd avoided the topic. Honestly, it had been hell even thinking of this time of year, since Kenzie had died so close to her favourite holiday.

"YES!!!!" she screamed, her eyes lighting up! "I can't wait!"

"What about you, sport?"

Tommy nodded as he drank his juice.

"Okay, it's a date. Get your homework done." I winked as I took the last couple bites of my chicken, sat back, and watched my kids.

"Alright, guys, out you go," I said, pulling up in front of the school, waiting while the kids gathered their things before getting out of the car.

"Tommy, you have your lunch, right?" I questioned, looking in the rear-view mirror at my son.

"He better. I put it in his bag this morning," Claire said, grabbing her schoolbag and throwing it over her shoulder, then looking over at her younger brother as he grinned up at her. "I swear, if you took it out of there, you're on your own," Claire said.

"Tommy, stop bugging your sister and check your bag, please. Last thing I need is a phone call from the school saying I didn't send a lunch."

"I got it," Tommy shouted as he looked inside his bag and zipped it back up.

"What about you?" I questioned, glancing at my watch to see I still had lots of time before I needed to be at the office.

"Lunch money," Claire said, holding up the twenty dollars I'd given her this morning.

"Spend it wisely." I winked. "Not on fries and junk."

"Dad, can't you just let me enjoy junk for once with my friends instead of shoving healthy food down my throat?" Claire said, rolling her eyes.

"Fine, but only today." I chuckled as she shut the door and then turned and smiled my way. Watching until I knew they were both safe inside, I pulled away from the sidewalk and toward work.

I stopped on my way at The Cooling Rack for a coffee and just as I pulled into the hospital parking lot, rain started coming down. I looked up at the sky, hoping that snow was in the forecast for the Christmas market, or I knew Claire and Tommy would be disappointed.

With hot coffee in my hand, I made my way toward

the hospital. I was just about to the employee entrance when Amelia came rushing around the corner, almost banging the coffee from my hand.

"Whoa," I said, pulling my coffee into the air, "slow down there."

"Sorry about that," she muttered as she looked up from her phone. Those pretty cinnamon eyes of hers met mine.

When she wasn't opening her mouth and giving me a snarky attitude all day, she reminded me of Kenzie. I held the door open for her and waited for her to step inside.

She looked up at me with shock, then stepped through the door, shifting her purse to the other hand as she turned and smiled up at me.

"Thank you, Dalton."

Even the way she said my name reminded me of my late wife. There was nothing I could do. I had to walk away. So, ignoring her, I pulled open the next door and once again waited until she walked through, then turned to make my way down a different hallway. I didn't believe in following my nurses to the office, anyway; I preferred to make my way into my office on my own.

"That would be when you're supposed to say you are welcome!" Sshe yelled in my direction.

I held my hand up and waved without looking back. As I continued down the hall, I finally heard her stomp her foot on the floor and let out a huff. That was when I turned to see her march on down the hall the way she'd been going, and I smiled to myself.

There were times I loved seeing her get all riled up. Somehow, it added enjoyment to my day. Like I said, she was a pretty woman, and for whatever reason, getting under her skin was something I looked forward to. I wasn't sure if it was the fact that she even acted like my precious Kenzie when she'd get upset with me or if it was because there was no one in this entire hospital in the past three years that had ever thought to stand up to me. I was hoping it was the latter, and not the fact that I was certain I was crushing on my nurse.

Amelia

My head pounded as I made my way to the cafeteria. The lights flickered as another crack of thunder and flash of lightning boomed across the sky.

"Ugh, isn't it supposed to be snowing?" I whined, coming up beside Charlotte, who had come in today to do some volunteer work for the staff Christmas party.

"You are in luck. It's in the forecast. Supposed to drop a couple inches by Friday, then it will finally look like Christmas." She smiled, looking at me. "Another headache?"

"Yeah, I already took some headache medicine, but I'm thinking this one just might be the beginnings of a migraine setting in."

"Hopefully not. How's Dalton today?"

I rolled my eyes. "God, he's impossible. Maybe worse than he was yesterday in the emergency room. Honestly, I don't know how much more of him I can take. He's just so…toxic. Did you know he is the only doctor in the entire hospital who hasn't decorated his office for Christmas? I noticed that this morning when I came in. I feel bad for our patients. Honestly, I'm tempted to bring in some decorations for the desk. You should do the same."

She smiled. "I worked for someone like that at the last hospital I was at. It's draining, that is for sure, especially at this time of the year."

"He's just so doom and gloom all the time. Doesn't he know this is supposed to be the most wonderful time of the year? He should be singing 'Jingle Bells' and smiling all the time. If not for his own peace of mind and mental health, then for the health and wellbeing of our patients. Thank God I have you to laugh with."

"I know. At least we make our own fun." She laughed.

I grabbed an apple and placed it on my tray, then an egg salad sandwich and a chocolate bar, followed by a soda.

"Although, we should remember that the holidays aren't the same for everyone, but I agree the office could use a little holiday spirit," she said, eyeing the food on my tray. "I haven't seen you ingest that much sugar in a while, especially with a headache."

I was normally a healthy eater, but today I was craving junk food. Dalton had tested my patience in more ways than one. Not only was I irritated, but it felt like someone was squeezing my head in a vise, and it didn't help that I was feeling highly emotional because most of the time my food choices reflected that.

"Yeah, I know. I shouldn't, but I can't help it." I shrugged. "Not today."

"Try to put a smile on that beautiful face." She giggled. "I know...it's that bad."

"I am," I said as we both laughed at her last comment, as I looked down at my sugar loaded tray.

We stepped up to the register, and we both paid, then we said our goodbyes and I went and sat down at an empty table in the cafeteria's corner. I needed to unwind and try to get rid of this headache before I went back to deal with my grump of a boss.

I cracked open my soda, took a bite of my sandwich, and began checking emails when I heard a high-pitched scream. I glanced up to see a young girl standing in the centre of the cafeteria, her hair an absolute disaster, her cheeks red and tear stained.

I frowned, wondering what was going on, and almost immediately I had my answer when she stepped to the side and I saw none other than Dalton sitting at the table. No doubt he was the cause of why she was acting this way.

I rolled my eyes. Dalton was everywhere I was, even in the breakroom. I watched from a distance as the young girl stomped her foot and pointed to her head and started crying. I'd had enough.

Dalton looked panicked as he looked around the room. He didn't know what to do, and if people weren't staring, I'd have probably just sat there and watched everything unfold. I was interested to see how the man who caused chaos in my life daily would handle the chaos this young girl was causing him. However, when she screamed again, my head almost exploded, so instead of just sitting there and watching, I got up from my seat and made my way over to where he sat, trying to calm the girl down with no luck.

"Dalton, I couldn't help but overhear...is there anything I can do to help?" I questioned, looking down at the young girl's tear-filled eyes.

One look at her told me she must be his daughter, and one look from him told me I was interrupting this special father-daughter bonding moment.

"Not now, Amelia," he barked, then focused his attention on his daughter.

"Claire, I don't know what you want me to do about this," he said back to the young girl who broke down into tears again.

Ignoring his orders like I normally did, I knelt down

beside her and turned her toward me before she let out another one of those nails-on-the-chalkboard screeching screams.

"What's wrong, sweetheart?" I questioned, looking up into her tear-filled eyes.

She looked at her father first and then at me. Wiping her eyes, she let out a sigh.

"I wanted to get my hair done at the same place my friend went to, but Dad chose the place instead and look at what they did. It's a disaster. I have a dance tonight, and I can't go like this. The kids will make fun of me. It's never gonna look right, and it's all his fault."

I glanced over at Dalton, who was watching me. He looked angry that I'd disobeyed him, but he clearly did not know how to fix this issue.

"I don't think your dad did this," I said, meeting his eyes.

He shrugged at me.

"He picked the salon." She sobbed.

I held my hand out toward him, hopefully signalling him to not say anything, as Claire wrapped her arms around me and cried against me.

"It's okay," I said, turning my attention back to her. "I could help you if you like. We could head over to the washroom. I have some things in my locker that I can use to fix your hair," I said.

She lifted her head, and those tear-filled eyes stared back at me. "Really?"

I nodded. "Yep, we can get you looking perfect in no time." I smiled.

"Can I, Dad?" she asked. "Please?"

Dalton just glared at me, not saying anything.

"Come, sweetheart," I said, gently placing my arm around her and guiding her toward the locker room. I knew if I gave Dalton time to answer, she'd more than likely have a meltdown. I knew how the man worked. He took pleasure in saying no.

"Amelia, she'll be fine. She's overreacting," I heard Dalton say as we walked away.

I ignored him as I heard him call my name again. We continued on to the locker room, where I helped her climb up on the counter before getting my things from my locker. I quickly started working on her hair. Twenty minutes later, I had her cute new hairstyle brushed out and styled.

"Wow!" she said excitedly as she hopped off the counter and glanced at herself in the mirror.

"You like?" I questioned.

"Very much. Thank you, Amelia," she said, wrapping her arms around my waist. "You should be a hairdresser!"

"You are welcome. Now for one finishing touch. How about a spritz of hairspray?"

The young girl looked up at me. "I'd like that, doubt my dad will."

I smiled and carefully sprayed her hair with a couple of spritzes. A part of me cheered inside, knowing that Dalton would probably hate it.

"There you go." I smiled before carefully putting my things back into the small bag I carried them in for emergencies.

The young girl studied herself in the mirror and then turned to me. "Thank you, Amelia."

"You are welcome, Claire. Now, how about we head back to where your father is and you can show him?"

"How did you do this?" she questioned, while I quickly washed my hands.

"Ah, just things you learn as a girl." I smiled. "You will learn eventually as well."

Sadness fell over her face as Claire looked in the mirror. "Oh," she whispered.

"What is it?"

"Did you learn those things from your mom?"

I smiled and nodded. "I did."

It was then I noticed her eyes watered. "Oh. I wish I had a mom to teach me those things."

A wave of guilt and shock rolled through me at the same time as I looked down at this little girl, who finally looked up at me and smiled. Was Dalton divorced? Was their mother not a part of their lives? Did she run out on her children? Then I thought back to the other night, at the words I spewed at Dalton, and I swallowed hard, for once feeling guilty at how horrible I'd been in that moment.

"Well, Claire, if you ever need anything, I'd be happy to help you. I work with your dad, so you can always reach me at the office." I winked.

I opened the door and held it while Claire ran out and right over to Dalton, who was standing across the hall from the women's locker room. He took a couple of moments with Claire, hugged her, and watched as she ran off toward an older woman who stood there with a young boy.

I smiled as I watched their exchange and then turned to head back to the cafeteria and finish my lunch just as Dalton locked eyes with me. The look in his eyes differed this time from how he normally looked at me. It was softer, lighter, almost as if he were smiling.

I gave him what I was sure was a confused smile. It was almost as if there was now a human component to him for the first time since I'd met him, and I was really unsure how to take it. As we stood there looking at one another, I almost felt as if he were looking into my soul. I swallowed hard, nodded, and walked back to the cafeteria when I heard him call my name.

I stopped and glanced over my shoulder at him.

"Amelia, I just want to say, thank you."

Shock at his words ran through me.

Without another word, he opened the door to the stairwell and was gone. I stood there, not sure what to do or how to accept what had just happened. In those mere seconds, for the first time, I finally glimpsed a completely different man.

Dalton

I STARED at the wall in front of me, the tip of my pen resting on my lip. I'd not been able to get this afternoon out of my head. Watching Amelia deal with Claire had done something to me.

When she'd first approached us, I wanted her to leave, but then watching her actually care enough to help my daughter opened something inside of me I hadn't felt in a while. I already knew she had a compassionate side, and she already reminded me so much of my Kenzie, and that action right there had only added to it.

After all, it was me and my child, and Amelia hated me with a passion and would do anything and everything to irritate. After she told me off the other night, I figured she'd apologize and beg for my forgiveness because she is always all about please and thank you and I'm sorry, but she still hadn't apologized. Her words that night had hit me, and they'd hit me hard. I hadn't realized how distant I'd become with my patients, my staff and coworkers, and even with my own kids. I really didn't know how to deal with anything anymore.

I made my way through the cafeteria line, picking up a few items and placing them on the tray, then I made my way up to the cashier and quickly paid for them, asking for everything to be put in a bag.

I walked through the hospital, over to the emergency department, and ran right into Sawyer.

"Hey, Dalton, what's up? Figured you'd be home by now." He glaced at the bag I carried.

"I would be, but I had to deliver this first. Is Amelia here still?" I questioned. "She, um, she forgot this in the office, and I wanted to bring it to her before I locked the door," I lied.

"Yep, she's behind the desk, or at least was when I was down there."

"Thanks, have a good night."

Sawyer looked at me with a confused expression. "Ah, you too, Dalton."

After returning from lunch, Amelia worked in the office for about half an hour before coming to my office and knocking on the door. When I looked up, she notified me she was planning to finish out her shift today in the emergency department if I didn't need her for anything. It had come as a surprise. She'd been one of the most steady and loyal employees I'd had, only ever taking a shift in another department when they were overrun. Otherwise, she'd find things to do in my office.

I'd granted her permission, but only because I figured the department was slammed and Sawyer had asked her to help like he normally did. Only it was quiet.

I rounded the corner and saw her sitting typing away on the computer. I walked over and placed the bag of food on the desk beside her. Getting her dinner was the least I could do for helping with Claire.

Startled, Amelia looked up at me.

"What is that??" she questioned, glancing at the bag and back to me.

"Well, you were kind enough to help Claire this morning during your break, and it's getting close to dinnertime. I thought you might be hungry, so I grabbed you something to eat for your last break. Just sort of payback." I shrugged.

"I didn't do it for you, or for compensation," she said, letting out a huff before slamming the pen she held down on the desk.

"It's not compensation." I frowned.

"Then what is it? Because that is what it feels like, and you said it was payback."

"Amelia, it was a simple thank you. One I think you should accept, and you will accept it."

"Always so bossy," she muttered.

Our eyes locked for a moment and then I broke away, heading back out of the emergency area, completely bugged that she'd actually think I'd try to pay her for helping.

"Dalton," I heard from behind me and glanced over my shoulder to see Amelia following me.

"Look, just accept the food," I said, spinning around and facing her.

She halted and looked at me. "I don't appreciate being told what I'm going to do or not do. I helped her because I genuinely cared, and for you to think otherwise of me is just...it's just...well, it's not fair."

She went to push past me, but I stopped her, grabbing her arms and holding her in front of me.

"Amelia, I thought nothing other than that. It actually shocked me."

"It shocked you I'd want to help someone?" she questioned. "I'm in the medical field, Dalton. Helping people is what I do."

"It shocked me because I know how you feel about me."

She frowned as she met my eyes. "What is that supposed to mean?"

"Amelia, just stop, okay? I know you can't stand me. I don't need that to be written for me to understand it. I see the way you look at me, the things you do to irritate me. I just think the fact that you helped her just...it was really nice is all, and honestly, in case you couldn't tell, I needed the help. It meant a lot, she um...she doesn't have a woman in her life to help her with these sorts of things. I do my best, but let's be honest, there are just things a girl needs her mother for."

"I agree. That was why I told her that if she needed anything, she could always call me."

"If that is the case, then I insist you keep the lunch."

"Again, Dalton, I didn't do this for any type of compensation. I meant what I said to her."

"I know."

She looked up at me with those beautiful eyes and swallowed hard. We stood there for what felt like minutes, looking at one another, until she broke eye contact. She cleared her throat and looked up at me once again.

"Despite what you might think, Dalton, I don't hate you."

"You don't?"

"No, and I'd never tell a child I'd be there for them if I didn't mean it. So, thank you for the food. I'll see you tomorrow."

She pushed past me and headed into the ladies' room. I stood there, shocked at her words. Did she actually just say what I thought she said? She didn't hate me? I swallowed hard as I stared at the door to the women's washroom.

Amelia

Snow was softly falling as I carried my hot chocolate and wandered around the small holiday market. It was a beautiful morning, and I'd taken advantage of my day off to do some Christmas shopping.

I took a sip of my hot chocolate and stopped at a fudge stand, choosing my flavours just as my phone rang. I quickly selected the last two flavours and handed the vendor the cash while I answered my phone. I hoped it wasn't work. I'd already put in the allowable amount of overtime for this month, and if it was, I'd have to turn down the shift. It wasn't something I liked to do, but it would be something I'd have to do, unless Connie would approve the overtime.

"Hello!" I sang into the receiver.

I heard a throat clear and then a cough. "Amelia?"

"This is she," I said, not recognizing the voice.

I heard whispering, followed by a throat clearing, followed by more whispering.

"Um, it's Dalton. I mean Doctor Frost. I mean Dalton."

I frowned. He sounded nervous and unsure of himself, which wasn't like him. I worried I'd missed a meeting or something because I couldn't figure out why else he'd be calling. It was his day off as well, so I knew it couldn't be work related.

"Yes? Is there something I can help you with?" I questioned.

"I'm so sorry to bother you on your day off...but I needed to ask you something."

"It's okay, but I will, um, have to get you the answers tomorrow once I'm in the office," I answered. "I'm not much good without my notes and the client files in front of me, I'm afraid."

"It's not work related," he said, his voice shaking. "I guess you could say it's more of a personal issue."

I frowned. A personal issue. Dalton didn't seem to be the type of person to need help in his personal life. I listened, curious to find out what he could want.

It was then I heard Claire in the background and then a muffled response from Dalton.

"I see. Well, what is it you need?" I questioned,

frowning as I listened to muffled voices again, certain Claire must need something.

"Sorry about the interruption. I have a favour to ask. I'm wondering if you could spare a little time today to come and see Claire. She has a bit of a problem and would like to speak with another woman, as she puts it."

I softly smiled. Claire was a sweet girl, and if she needed someone, there was no way I'd turn her down. I'd hold up my promise.

"Sure, I can. I just need the address," I said, glancing at my watch.

"75 Sycamore," Dalton replied.

"Okay, um, I should be able to be there within the next couple of hours," I answered.

"Great, thank you, Amelia."

"No problem."

I'D TAKEN my time finishing up at the holiday market before heading home to get ready. I showered, pulled my hair back in a bun, and quickly did my makeup before I hopped into my car and made my way over. I pulled up outside the two-story home, put my car in park, and cut the engine. Grabbing my purse, I made my way to the front door, careful not to slip on the snow-covered walkway.

I was about to knock when the door opened abruptly, and there stood Dalton. At first, I thought I was at the wrong house and looked up to make sure it was the right place. I barely recognized him. He wore blue jeans and a T-shirt, and I couldn't help but notice he was barefoot. He looked so different dressed in casual clothing.

"Amelia, thank you so much for coming over," he said, an actual smile on his face.

Where is Dalton Frost and what have you done with him, I thought to myself as I stared at this incredibly sexy man. That was the only thing running through my mind as I stepped into his house and he closed the door behind me.

"I hope you didn't mind me calling you. Claire has been having a terrible morning. Mrs. Jenkins would normally deal with her, but she is on her weekend off and, well, I didn't want to call her, but I didn't know what to do. She insisted she couldn't talk to me about it. She claimed it was a woman's issue."

I smiled, almost laughed. It sounded funny that she wouldn't talk to her father about a woman's issue, considering he was a gynecologist.

"What's so funny?' he questioned.

"I think you know what is funny," I added as I followed behind him, glancing into the living room as we walked through into the kitchen where I found Claire sitting at the kitchen table, her cheeks flushed, her eyes red. Had she been crying?

"Hey, Claire," I said, smiling down at her.

"Amelia, you came!" she said, jumping up and running over to me, wrapping her arms around my waist.

"What's going on?" I questioned, giving her a one-armed hug.

I glanced over at Dalton, who stood there, coffee mug in his hand, watching us. He leaned up against the counter, and for the first time, I noticed how his muscles flexed in his forearms and how strong his hands were. I'd worked with this man daily for a year and had noticed none of this before. When I looked back down at Claire, I noticed she glanced over to Dalton and then back at me.

"Can we go talk in private?" she whispered.

I looked back over to Dalton, who cleared his throat. I was expecting him to force her to talk to me here, but he surprised me.

"You can use the backyard if you like." He nodded, gently smiling at Claire.

"Thanks." I looked down at Claire, who slipped her hand into mine and led me to the backdoor.

Once outside, Claire nodded to four empty chairs in the middle of the backyard. I followed her over, and we both took a seat.

"So, what is going on that you can't talk to your dad about?" I questioned.

Her cheeks flushed, and she shook her head. "It's embarrassing," she mumbled.

"Okay, well, how about you just take a deep breath and tell me?" I smiled.

Claire did as I suggested and, without looking at me, she murmured, "I woke up this morning and there was blood in my bed," she said, almost near tears.

I gently smiled, remembering when I'd gotten my first period. It was almost identical to what had happened to Claire. The only difference was I had my mother to talk about it with.

"Mrs. Jenkins wasn't here, and I couldn't tell my dad." Tears filled her eyes.

"It's okay. No need to cry. I can help you with this, no problem." I smiled, reaching into my purse and pulling out a pad. "You've gone over these things in health class, I take it?"

Claire nodded. "I just had nothing in the house, and I didn't want to ask Dad to take me to the drugstore because I'd rather die. I was going to wait until Monday when Mrs. Jenkins was here, but I wasn't sure I should."

"No problem. How about I take you to the drugstore? We can get you some supplies and you can ask me all the questions you'd like to ask in private. Sound good?"

Claire nodded, smiling at me. "Thank you."

"No problem. Now why don't you head on up to

your room, get ready, and I will take you to the drugstore."

"Okay," she said, getting up from the chair and shoving the pad into the pocket of her jeans. "Oh, and, Amelia?"

"Yes?"

"Don't tell my dad, okay?"

I flinched a little, not sure I really wanted to keep something like that from her father. I softly smiled. "Honey, don't you worry. I will talk with your dad, but I'm almost certain he will understand. He deals with this stuff every day at work. There is nothing to be ashamed of."

"I know. I just don't want him to know."

I softly smiled. "It's okay, I will talk with him," I assured her. "Now go on and get ready."

I gave her a moment to head into the house and then got up and made my way inside, where I found Dalton still in the kitchen, still barefoot, drinking his coffee.

"Everything okay?" he questioned the moment I came inside.

"Yes, everything is fine," I answered.

Without asking, he poured me a cup of coffee and placed it down in front of me, which I gladly accepted and took a sip.

"She really had me worried. She's never refused to speak to me before."

I walked over beside him and looked out the back window out to the sprawling yard I'd just sat in.

"She doesn't want you to know, but you need to. She got her period," I said.

Almost immediately, Dalton's cheeks flushed as he tore his eyes from mine. "I see. Well, that definitely called for needing another woman."

I'd never seen him act this way before. "Are you okay?" I questioned.

"Yep, thanks for coming over," he said, swallowing hard.

"Dalton, are you embarrassed? You deal with these things for a living."

Dalton met my eyes. "Not embarrassed. Guess I forgot how old she really was. Most days I look at them and still see them as five years old."

"Gotcha. Well, I told her I'd take her over to the drugstore and get her some supplies."

Dalton looked at me, relief washing over his face. I was about to ask him if he was okay when I heard footsteps coming down the stairs. I glanced at him.

"Say nothing." I whispered.

"My lips are sealed," he whispered back, gently smiling.

"Ready to go?" I questioned, turning to see Claire standing on the other side of the island.

"Yes," she answered.

I made my way around the island and began following her to the front door when Dalton cleared his throat and called my name. We both turned to look at him.

"I was wondering if perhaps you might like to join us for dinner tonight?"

"Oh, well, I—"

"Please, Amelia!" Claire begged.

I smiled at her and then looked over at Dalton. I really didn't know how to take this at all. First, he was more human than I'd ever seen, and second, he was inviting me into his home to have dinner with him and his kids.

"I mean, if you already have plans, I understand. I just thought it might be nice..."

"Say no more." I smiled. "I'll stay."

"Yay!" Claire screamed.

I couldn't help but laugh as I listened to Claire and how excited she was for me to be staying for dinner as I followed her through the house and out to my car.

***

DALTON HAD ORDERED in from The Golden Lotus, a new Thai restaurant in Eastport. During dinner, Claire and Tommy shared stories about their week at school and about some of their favourite hobbies. Once the food was gone, the table cleared and dishes were done, Dalton made us a coffee and left me in the living room while he went to tuck both kids into bed.

I now sat in the living room, sipping on the hot coffee, flipping through a magazine while I waited for him.

"Sorry about that. Tommy wouldn't stop talking about that one kid at school that invited him for the weekend to the cottage," Dalton said, coming over and sitting down on the couch beside me.

"Not a problem." I smiled. "He seemed pretty excited about the invite at dinner, too."

"Yeah, that is Tommy. I haven't even given him a yes or no yet." Dalton chuckled.

"Well, I hope it's a yes, otherwise I think he is going to be pretty upset," I said, thinking back to how excited he looked.

Dalton chuckled. I wasn't sure I'd ever even heard the man laugh before. Dalton was good-looking. I'd always thought so, and he had a really pleasant smile too, and there was a glint in his eyes as he looked at me. Today was the first time I'd seen a personality to match the total package.

The room grew quiet as we looked at one another, and soon his sombre face returned. I swallowed hard as I placed my mug down on the table.

"Well, thank you once again for dinner. Really, you didn't have to," I said, reaching for my purse.

"It was my way of saying thank you for helping me with Claire."

"Like I said before, you don't need to thank me," I said, feeling annoyed as I dug into my purse for my keys. Finally, I felt them and looked over at Dalton, ready to announce my departure.

"Like I said before, I know you don't like me very much," he said. "In fact, I'm almost sure you probably hate me."

I frowned and sat back, looking over at him. He seemed almost vulnerable.

I placed my keys back down on top of my purse, waiting for him to talk, but he just studied me.

"Like I said before, I don't hate you. I don't have room in my heart for hate. I will say I don't like the way you treat people."

I could tell from the look on his face he knew how he was treating people was wrong, which if he knew that, then I wondered why he continued.

"I think I'm going to head home," I said, shifting myself to the edge of the couch to stand when he grabbed my hand. I looked down to where his hand rested on my arm and then over at his face.

"I...I didn't use to be this way," he murmured. "So short and cold with people."

I could tell from the look on his face that whatever he was about to say was serious and that he needed to share whatever it was. I shifted on the couch and turned my hand around so his rested on mine.

"What happened?" I questioned.

"It was November, snowing bad. I was working nights in the emergency. It was a busy night. Claire had called to say good night right as the EMTs brought in two stabbing victims and a car accident. Immediately, I took the accident, saying good night to Claire. I rushed over to the room where they were working to get the patient stable."

As I watched him, I noticed the colour had drained from his face and knew immediately what he was going to say, but I let him continue, not wanting to stop him. He obviously needed someone to talk to, and if I was that someone he was comfortable sharing with, then I'd be the ear.

"I shoved the curtain to the side and began reading over the extent of the injuries. Broken leg, possible broken pelvis, broken ribs, oxygen levels were low, suggesting maybe a punctured or collapsed lung, possible internal bleeding as well. As I made my way to the head of the stretcher and looked down at the woman who lay there, my world stopped. Every ounce of air that had been in the room was gone, the room spinning out of control as I looked down at my wife."

I closed my eyes, blinking away the burning feeling that was certain to become tears. I couldn't imagine how he must have felt at that moment.

"In that moment, the noise of the emergency room fell away and every memory my mind held flashed before me. The first time we met, the first time we kissed, the first time we...our first home, our first baby, our second baby....the trip we'd just taken to Hawaii. Panic filled me and the room continued to spin out of control. That was when I turned and vomited on the floor. I couldn't ever remember a time that I couldn't breathe, couldn't even think. All I could see was her beautiful face laying on that stretcher as I sunk to my knees in shock. The RN who I normally worked with immediately noticed and she came over and that was when they called the code."

"Oh, Dalton..." I whispered, my eyes filling with tears as I gripped his hand a little tighter.

"It literally felt like hours as they worked on her, not minutes, as it truly was."

Dalton fell quiet as we both sat there. The look of heartbreak combined with sadness pulled at my heart. It wasn't a wonder the man was the way he was. He'd suffered not only a devastating loss, but had seen it with his own eyes. It would cause the warmest, caring person to turn inward.

"When I heard that flatline, I knew my entire world was about to change, only it didn't just change, it literally stopped."

My heart hurt for Dalton and for Claire and Tommy.

"Dalton, I'm sorry, I did not know."

"I wouldn't have expected you to," he quietly answered.

Almost immediately, I remembered all those horrible things I'd said to him that afternoon when I'd lost my composure. How horrible he was, how his significant other must hate being around such a grumpy man. Those words were now that bitter pill I had to swallow and made me feel like a fool.

"I think I'm going to get going," I said, swallowing hard, wishing I'd never said those words to him.

Dalton nodded and whispered, "I understand."

"Before I do, I want to apologize for all the things—"

He placed his forefinger on my lips, silencing me. "No need. They needed to be said," he whispered, meeting my eyes.

Embarrassment and anger flooded me. They didn't need to be said. I should have been fired over those words. I'd overstepped. I'd attacked his personal life, and that wasn't professional in the slightest.

I grabbed my purse and keys and made my way to the front door where I slipped my shoes on. I could barely breathe at the thought of my words from that night.

When I turned to say goodbye, I didn't expect Dalton to be right there. His body was so close to me, I could feel the heat pouring off it. His eyes met mine, and I felt him take my hand in his.

I had no idea what was happening inside me at the

moment. I wanted him to kiss me. I wanted to know what his lips would feel like against mine. I wanted him to take me in his arms and pull me against him. I wanted to feel his body against mine, but most of all I wanted to take his pain away, if only for a moment or two.

My heart pounded as I studied his eyes and silence fell between us. The longer I stood there, the warmer I felt, and the realization that I was about to cross a professional line was staring me in the face.

"I'll see you tomorrow at work," I whispered, as something in my brain forced me to stop thinking that way.

"Good night, Amelia."

"Night, Dalton."

Amelia

"CAROL, if you'd like to come with me, I'll get you set up in one of the treatment rooms," Charlotte said, taking the file folder from the pile I'd just placed on the desk.

The lady smiled at me as she passed the desk and followed Charlotte down the hall.

It was Friday. It had been five days since I'd been at Dalton's house, and he'd barely even spoken to me. I went back to the file I was working on when Dalton came around the corner and dropped a file folder down in front of me without so much as a word, and then went to go back down the hall when he stopped.

"Amelia, call Mrs. Johnson and share with her the results of her tests," he grunted.

I stopped what I was doing and looked up at Dalton. I'd seen Mrs. Johnson's test results this morning, and it wasn't good news. I knew she'd have questions, as would anyone with a cancer diagnosis. I also knew I shouldn't be answering them.

"Wait," I said, loud enough to get the attention of some patients in the waiting area.

"What?" Dalton barked and rolled his eyes.

Charlotte stepped out of the treatment room she'd just put Carol into and looked at the pair of us, wondering what was going on.

"Can I speak with you in private, please?" I questioned, looking up at him.

I could see the annoyance in his eyes as I continued down the hall and entered his office, waiting for him.

I was looking out the window when I heard his door click shut.

"What is it? If you pulled me in here to tell me you don't want to call Mrs. Johnson, that is too bad. I have asked you to do it, and I'm not taking no for an answer," he sternly replied.

Dalton had been in a terrible mood for most of the week. He'd worked late every night, well past his usual time. I'd have thought that after he'd shared things about his wife with me, he'd have been different, but I'd been wrong about that too.

"What is wrong?" I questioned, cutting right to the chase instead of dancing around it.

"Nothing."

"Oh no, Dalton, it's not nothing. You have been horrendous lately. Worse than usual. Poor Charlotte has been afraid to do anything, and in case you didn't notice, no one even looked your way today while you were in the cafeteria. People are avoiding you more than ever."

"Good, I'm glad they are avoiding me. They at least know what is good for them, unlike you."

I crossed my arms and glared at him. This was Dalton at work. This wasn't the man I'd shared dinner with less than a week ago.

"Dalton, just stop. Now, something is wrong, because the man I shared dinner with—"

"Whoa, you shared dinner with me and my family, and that will be the end of that talk. I don't need rumours spreading around the hospital about me fraternizing with one of my staff," he barked.

"There isn't a non-fraternization policy here, Dalton. Besides, just because two people share dinner together does not mean they are in a relationship of any kind aside from a friendship," I said. "So what gives?"

Dalton looked at me and then turned around. I saw his shoulders rise and fall in a deep sigh.

"Today is..."

His voice was barely audible, and I strained to hear what he was going to say next. I waited, only he said nothing.

"Today is what?" I questioned.

He was quiet, his shoulders rising and falling. "Today is the anniversary of my wife's death," he finally answered.

Heat flooded my body as his words hit me. What on earth was he doing here? He should be at home, spending time with the kids, learning how to deal or cope with whatever was running through his head.

"Why are you here? You should be at home with Claire and Tommy," I cried, realizing that those kids were alone.

"I can't," he quietly murmured.

"You can't? Why not?" I questioned. "Your children need you. They need to be with you, not be alone, or with their nanny."

"You don't understand."

I crossed my arms over my chest. He was right; I didn't understand, but I knew those children needed their father probably more today than ever, and it was bloody selfish of him to be here with his patients than to be at home allowing those kids to cope.

"What I understand is that you are being an ass," I bit out.

Dalton whipped around and looked at me. The look in his eyes almost ripped my heart out.

"I can't be there for my kids, because I do not know how to even handle how I feel, never mind how they feel."

I saw the vulnerability in his eyes and immediately wanted to hug him. Once again, I wanted to take away his pain because it was more than obvious to me he was definitely in pain, only I didn't dare. Who knew how he'd react?

"If you will excuse me, I have patients I need to see," he said and turned and stepped out of the office, leaving me there alone.

***

I'D JUST HUNG up the phone when Dalton dropped another patient file on my desk and left the office . He took off across the hall and stood at the elevator, pressing the button.

I turned to Charlotte. "I'll be back in a few minutes, just going to grab a coffee."

"Sure."

I grabbed my purse and took off out of the clinic and over to the elevator where Dalton stood. I was about to say something when the elevator door opened. We both stepped inside and waited for the door to close.

"What time is your shift over?" I questioned.

"Why?"

"Well, I've been thinking. If it's the same time mine ends, how about I go with you home?"

I stood there, my stomach in knots, waiting for his answer. He was quiet for so long, I figured I'd hear about this later today before I left the office. He probably thought I was trying to come on to him or something and would probably ask me to clean out my desk and not to return.

"Why would you offer to do that?" he asked. "We aren't friends."

I thought for a moment, unsure how to answer him. He needed someone, that much I knew. I knew I could be that someone for him, if he'd let me. He'd opened up once before.

"Dalton, we don't have to be friends for me to help you and your family, but I'd like us to be."

The elevator stopped, and the door opened. Dalton looked at me, then took off without another word. I would not chase him. In fact, I wouldn't say another word about this ever again. It was the only time I was offering. I pressed the button for the eighth floor and took off back to the office.

I JUST FILED the last of the medical files away and grabbed my coat from the hook, then bent down and pulled my purse from the bottom drawer of the desk.

I'd been on edge ever since I'd returned from talking with Dalton in the elevator. He hadn't said a word to me when he returned. We just went about our day as if nothing had happened.

I let out a sigh and went to shut the light off when my hand collided with another hand, causing me to jump.

"Sorry I didn't see you there," I heard a deep voice say and looked up to see Dalton standing there in his coat, his laptop bag flung over his shoulder.

"It's okay," I said, swallowing hard. "I guess I'll see you tomorrow." I gave him a small smile.

He didn't move, so I stepped out from behind the desk and made my way to the clinic door and was about to push it open when I heard him clear his throat behind me.

"Amelia?"

I glanced over my shoulder at him, not saying a word, just waiting for him to speak.

"I just wanted to let you know that I'm sorry about this afternoon."

I nodded. "Of course."

"It's just that your offer took me by surprise, and I didn't really know what to say. If your offer is still on the table, I'd like it if you would join us for dinner tonight."

I could tell from the look on his face that it took a lot for him to apologize and to ask me to join them.

"I don't know how to be with my kids today," he whispered.

I stood in Dalton's kitchen ripping up lettuce for the Caesar salad while he stirred the pot that contained the pasta before moving to the one that held the sauce.

"Do you have any croutons?" I questioned.

"Yep, in the pantry," he said. "Second or third shelf."

We'd been here almost an hour, had said goodbye to Mrs. Jenkins, and hadn't seen the kids once. The house was eerily quiet, almost unsettling.

"Would you like a little music?" I questioned, looking at the small radio on the counter.

Dalton looked at me, then at the radio, and swallowed hard, but said nothing.

It was almost like the man was allergic to anyone having a good time.

"If not, that's okay," I said, grabbing the bag of croutons from the pantry. "Just thought it would add a little magic in the air. After all, Christmas is coming. Might make the kids come out of their rooms and join us."

"Go ahead," he said.

I smiled and turned the radio on. Christmas music flooded the kitchen with one of my favourite songs. I made my way back over to where I was working on the salad and finished ripping up the lettuce and was about to dump the croutons in when I heard a voice behind me.

"Amelia?"

I turned to see Claire standing there with her brother.

She smiled, but it didn't reach her eyes, and Tommy hid behind her, not smiling either.

"Hey, Claire!" I said, trying to sound upbeat for them. "Hi, Tommy."

"You're listening to the radio? Dad never—"

"Claire!" Dalton yelled in that familiar stern voice he usually used at the office, causing me to jump and dump half the box of croutons into the salad.

I glanced over at Claire to see tears fill her eyes, and then looked over at Dalton and shook my head.

"Guys, go get ready for dinner," Dalton barked, draining the pot of pasta into a strainer.

I looked over at Claire, her eyes filled with tears, and watched as she took Tommy and headed down the hall to the washroom.

"What was that?" I questioned.

"Is the garlic bread ready for the oven?" he asked, ignoring my question completely.

This time I ignored him and grabbed the tray with the garlic bread and shoved it into the oven.

IT WAS UNBEARABLY quiet at dinner. When Claire and Tommy both returned to the dining room, neither of them even looked my way. They sat there, eyes down, and ate. Dalton sat looking out the window, ignoring everyone. It was the most uncomfortable dinner I'd ever sat through, and wondered if this was what homelife for these kids had been like since their mother died.

The moment plates were empty, Dalton gathered them and carried them into the kitchen without a word to anyone. I looked at both the kids, my heart hurting for them.

"You both doing okay?" I asked quietly. "Your dad told me what today is."

Tommy looked up at me with red eyes. He'd been crying at some point. Probably before they came into dinner, and when Claire looked up at me, she had tears in her eyes.

"Did you guys want to talk about your mom?" I questioned, glancing at the doorway to the dining room.

Dalton was more than likely making coffee and cutting the cake I'd stopped to pick up on my way here. I didn't care if he overheard; he needed to overhear. He needed to be here for his kids. He should be the one asking these questions, not me, some stranger.

Claire looked at me. "I can sometimes still smell her perfume," she said, her voice barely audible. "It was my favourite. I still have a bit in a bottle she used to use. I don't use it, just smell it when I'm missing her."

"I did the same thing with a bottle of my father's cologne." I softly smiled. I wanted her to know there was nothing wrong with what she was doing, because there was no doubt in my mind that if Dalton had caught her, he'd have yelled.

"What about you, Tommy?"

He shrugged. "I don't remember much. I was so little. I sometimes get this song stuck in my head. Claire told me Mom used to sing it to me."

"Can you hum it for me?"

When he began humming it, I instantly recognized it. That was when Dalton walked in. He stood there, watching Tommy sitting there with his eyes closed, humming. He surprised me as he then looked at me and started saying the words.

"Baby mine, don't you cry. Baby mine, dry your eyes."

He placed the two mugs of coffee that were on the tray he carried in front of me and himself, then placed two glasses of milk in front of both the kids, all while continuing to say the words while Tommy hummed.

Claire looked at me with tears in her eyes. When Tommy stopped humming, he too looked up with tears in his eyes. I was almost certain I even saw Dalton's eyes water a little as he finished.

My throat was tight as I sat there witnessing something I'd never thought I would. Dalton bent down and placed a kiss on the top of both kids' heads, gave them a hug, and whispered something into each of their ears before he sat down and took a sip of his coffee, and probably for the first time he actually started talking to his kids about their mother.

AFTER WE'D FINISHED dessert and Dalton shared some stories about his wife with the kids, it was time for them to get ready for bed. While he went up and tucked them in, I quickly cleaned up the kitchen and started the dishwasher, then poured us two fresh cups of coffee and made my way into the living room, where I sat down just as Dalton joined me.

"I poured you a fresh coffee," I said as he sat down beside me.

"Thank you," he said, grabbing the mug and taking a sip.

"No problem." I smiled.

"No, I mean for today. If it wasn't for you, well, I don't think I would have gotten through tonight."

"It wasn't a problem. Glad to help, but honestly, it was by sharing those stories with the kids that got you through it."

"Well, it meant a lot to me you were here," he whispered, his eyes washing over my face. "No one has ever cared enough..."

"That's because you don't let anyone in, Dalton. For people to care, they have to be allowed to get close to you."

"I'm afraid to let anyone in..."

His eyes studied mine, then they fell to my lips. I felt like we were getting closer, and I fought the urge to lean forward and place a kiss on his lips. It would be wrong.

I tore my eyes from his and looked down at the mug in my hands. I was about to say something when I felt his fingers under my chin. I slowly lifted my head and was surprised when he leaned forward. The room fell away as he placed his lips on mine and my fingers gently played with the hair on the back of his head. I could have easily allowed myself to get lost in him if he hadn't pulled away.

The room was silent. I could hear my heart beating and panic flooded me.

"I've got to get going," I said, jumping to my feet.

I had to get out of there. The second his lips touched mine, I wanted more. The emptiness I felt when he'd pulled away was almost unbearable.

"Amelia, wait..." Dalton said, standing as well. "I'm sorry, I shouldn't have..."

"Don't be silly. It's fine," I said, grabbing my purse and slipping my feet into my shoes, not sure if I was going to panic or kiss the man again.

I was about to pull the door open when I felt his hands on my upper arms. I froze, not able to move.

"Amelia..." he breathed.

"Dalton..."

"Yes?" he answered.

"It's been a long and emotional day. I think it's best if we both say good night."

I didn't wait; I opened the door and stepped out onto the porch, feeling Dalton's hands slip from my arms.

"Good night, Dalton. I'll see you on Monday."

I didn't look back; I rushed to my car, climbed in, and backed out of the driveway.

Dalton

I LET OUT a yawn as I was going over the notes from this morning's meeting. I'd barely slept the weekend after Amelia left. I felt like a complete fool. I'd kissed her, I'd let my guard down, something I'd promised myself would never happen. Then I'd tossed and turned all night, worrying that she was going to report me to human resources today, and if not today, I was sure it would only be a matter of time.

I let out a sigh and closed my notebook, glancing at the clock. It was almost one, and I'd still not seen Amelia today. She hadn't called in sick either, which was unlike her. I left my office and made my way down the hall toward the front desk, where I found Charlotte on the phone. I went into the copy room only to find it empty and then returned to the front desk.

"If you are looking for Amelia, they called and asked if she could come to the emergency room. Apparently, they were slammed, and we weren't, so I told her to go. You were in your meeting."

I nodded. Normally, she would have cleared it with me first, but she hadn't, which normally would have made me angry.

Charlotte looked up at me, waiting for my reaction. Only I had nothing to give. After the other night, I knew I was skating on thin ice.

"I'm going to head down for lunch. Want anything?"

Charlotte looked at me weirdly. What was the matter with me? This wasn't the cold exterior I normally had. I'd never offered to get my employees anything.

"No, I'm good, thanks," she said hesitantly, looking up at me with concern.

"Okay, be back soon," I said, heading toward the door.

Making my way into the cafeteria, I grabbed my lunch and was about to sit down at a quiet table off to the left side when I spotted Amelia sitting alone. I wanted to apologize again, so I approached her slowly. She had her headphones in and didn't notice me until I was almost beside her.

"Dalton, hi," she said, removing one of her earbuds. From what I could tell, she was annoyed with me.

"Mind if I join you?" I questioned, fully prepared for

her to tell me to take a hike, only she didn't. Instead, she smiled and nodded to the chair beside her.

"Please, sit down."

A funny feeling came over me as I sat down and opened my soda. "Amelia, I wanted to apologize again about Friday night. I was way out of line."

She placed her hand on mine and softly smiled. "Dalton, relax. It's okay, given everything that went on that night and what you were dealing with. It's understandable. We both know it was nothing more than a simple mistake."

I couldn't have her thinking that. It wasn't a mistake. It was something I'd wanted from the first time I laid eyes on her, and from the gentleness of her kiss back, the way her fingers ran through my hair at the back of my head, I guessed she'd wanted it as well.

"No."

She looked up at me with questions in her eyes.

"I knew what I was doing. It wasn't a mistake. I'm... I'm very attracted to you and have been for a long time," I said, closing my eyes, feeling a bit of relief rise off my chest.

"What?" Amelia questioned, her eyes meeting mine.

I was quiet for a while, not sure I was ready to tell her exactly how I was feeling. I knew I had to, but it was hard to get the words out.

"Amelia, I have feelings for you, and I have for a while."

Shock immediately flooded her face at my admission. Her cheeks went red, and I realized that the cafeteria probably wasn't the best place to admit this to her.

"Dalton, I—"

"I'm sorry, but if I'm not honest about this, then..."

She swallowed hard, and her eyes watered as she waited for me to continue, only I couldn't. The familiar feeling of choking, like all the air was being sucked from this room, hit me as I sat there waiting for the only thing that I figured was coming my way. Rejection.

"Dalton, please, we will talk about this later, in private," she said, throwing her half-eaten muffin down on her tray before standing up and grabbing her things, leaving me there alone.

Amelia

Amelia, I have feelings for you.

His words ran through my mind as I hooked up an IV for what I hoped would be the last patient of the day. I was exhausted, and my mind was in overdrive.

"Did you hear what I said?" I heard a woman say.

I looked down at the patient laying on the stretcher, certain there was nothing but confusion on my face.

"I'm sorry, what?"

"I said that hurts."

I looked down to see I was holding the needle a little crooked in her arm and immediately straightened it.

"Oh my gosh, I'm so sorry," I said, trying hard to focus and pay more attention to what I was doing than what I was thinking about. "Sorry about that."

"It's okay. I told you I have a little needle phobia, and I detest having IVs."

"Most people do," I said, placing a piece of tape across the back of her hand, securing the IV in place. "Honestly, I don't know if I have ever met someone who likes them, and I'm normally very good at setting the IV."

"Uh-huh," she said, looking away from me.

I turned on the machine and slipped from the room, depositing my gloves into the trash and my gown into the wash bin, then headed for the desk, where I finished up my notes. The moment I finished, Dalton's admission flooded my mind again.

I let out a sigh. Truth was, I'd been feeling the same way he did, and it hadn't helped that I'd always found him attractive, but since seeing a caring side to him, it had gotten worse. I'd done my best to shove my thoughts to the back of my mind, and it had worked, until we'd shared that kiss.

It was the last thing on my mind last night when I'd closed my eyes and the first thing I'd thought of when I'd opened them, and if I thought about it hard enough, I could still feel his lips on mine.

I finished making the last of my notes, and as soon as my replacement came in, I left, ready to head home for the night.

I was almost to the parking garage when I reached into my pocket, only to find my keys were missing. That was when I realized I'd left my purse upstairs in the office. I'd been called to the ER almost immediately after arriving and had just left everything there. I let out a sigh and made my way back to the hospital.

The lights were off in the office, which sent a sigh of relief through me. Everyone was already gone for the day. I swiped my key card and opened the door and made my way in behind the desk and opened the filing cabinet drawer, pulling my purse out from inside, then grabbed my jacket from the hook on the wall and slid into it. I turned around and went to take a step when I ran into someone and let out a scream.

"Amelia, it's okay. It's only me. Dalton."

I placed my hand on my chest, my heart was racing. "What are you still doing here?" I cried, trying to slow my breathing.

"I was just getting ready to leave. What are you doing here?"

"The same thing!" I exclaimed. "I left my purse and jacket here. I thought everyone was gone for the night."

"Same here." Dalton chuckled. "Look, I'm glad you are here. I'd like to take you out for dinner, so we can talk."

The look in his eyes was so genuine, and when he reached out and took my hand in his, all I could do was follow him.

WE SHARED a lovely and quiet dinner along with a bottle of wine at one of the best restaurants in Eastport. We talked about our day, laughing and joking, and then Dalton drove us back to his place. He slid his hand into mine as we drove back to his place and when we stepped into the house, two smiling faces and Mrs. Jenkins greeted us.

"What are you guys still doing up?" Dalton questioned, looking over to Mrs. Jenkins.

"We wanted to watch our show," Claire explained, getting up and coming over to me, wrapping her arms around me. "I'm so happy to see you."

"I'm happy to see you, too!" I exclaimed.

"Okay, guys, why don't you head on up and get ready for bed, and I'll be up in a minute," Dalton instructed.

"Can't Amelia tuck us in tonight?" Claire asked, and Tommy agreed.

Dalton looked over at me and then at both his kids and nodded. "Well, if it's okay with Amelia, sure."

"It's fine. Come on, kids, let's go."

I took them both upstairs and waited while they changed and brushed their teeth, then tucked each one of them into bed before making my way back downstairs. Soft music played on the living room speakers, and Dalton sat on the couch, two glasses of wine poured.

"They go down, okay?"

"Yep, Tommy was asleep the moment his head hit the pillow." I giggled.

Dalton smiled and patted the empty seat beside him. I went over and sat down as he handed me my glass of wine.

"Did you enjoy dinner?"

"Very much," I whispered, taking a sip of my wine.

Dalton took my hand in his and ran his thumb over the back of my hand. He was a completely different man than he was at work. This Dalton Frost I could easily see myself falling in love with. I met his eyes and softly smiled.

"Amelia, I know I'm not always the easiest man to get along with."

"Somehow, though, I can understand. You've been through a lot over the past few years."

"I have."

"I want to let you know that I'm sorry for what I said that night. I know I've apologized before, but if I had known about your wife, I'd never have said..."

He placed his forefinger on my lips, silencing me. "It's okay. Don't worry about it. I deserved it."

"Well, maybe in some ways, but you didn't deserve that comment."

"No, I probably did. Honestly, I probably deserved more than what you gave. I guess the reason I'm always worse to you than anyone else at the office is because you reminded me of Kenzie."

"Really?"

Dalton nodded. "Yes. I guess it scared me because when I first started noticing those things that you exhibit that had originally attracted me to her, my first instinct was to push you away."

I nodded, studying his eyes. He was guarded, which made sense. I could understand that too. If my world had been suddenly ripped from me, it would make me the same.

"Amelia, I've given a lot of thought to things over the past few weeks. I feel there could be something between us."

"What do you mean?" I questioned, taking a sip of my wine and averting my eyes for a moment.

"I mean, I think there could be something more between us than just co-workers and friends. I think I'd like us to explore that option. If you are interested, that is."

"Dalton, I'm not sure we should date. I mean, we work together. You are my boss."

Dalton was quiet for a moment. "You never mentioned work earlier. It didn't seem to bother you to come here and help Claire, or to have dinner with me before, so that is not what is bothering you. So, what is holding you back?"

His words ran through my mind. Being friends didn't

seem to be a problem with the work thing, but what would people think at work if we were dating? I hadn't exactly been silent about how I'd felt about Dalton, and even though my feelings were changing, the thought scared me a little.

He brought his hand to my cheek, and the moment his hand touched me, heat flooded my body. His eyes captivated me, and before I could stop myself, I leaned forward and met his lips.

"We can't be caught at work like this," I whispered.

"Not at work, I agree, but what we do in our personal life is no one's business," he whispered, bringing his lips back to mine.

His kiss this time was a little more demanding as he wrapped his arms around me and pulled me toward him. In one quick movement, he'd pulled me over so I was straddling his lap. As our kiss deepened, his hands gripped my ass and pulled me closer toward him. I could already feel him straining against his jeans. Every part of me was on fire, and I let out a soft moan as his hands began exploring my body.

One hand snaked into my hair, and he gently pulled as he kissed me again, sending waves of pleasure through me. I ran my fingers through the hair at the back of his head as he kissed his way down my neck and back up, nibbling on my ear.

"You like that?" he whispered.

The feel of his breath on my neck and ear sent chills through me, causing my centre to throb.

"Very much so." I moaned.

Cupping my cheek, he brought his lips to mine again, kissing me slow. A bolt of excitement ran through me when I felt his hand slide under my shirt and brush against my stomach in a tender touch. I pulled away, studying his eyes, then gripped the bottom of my shirt and pulled it off over my head.

I craved his lips but loved watching his eyes as they ran over my body, stopping on my breasts. I reached behind me and unclipped my bra, letting it fall away from my body. He immediately grabbed me, pulling me forward, his mouth meeting my breast. I felt his tongue flick my hard nipple as he sucked the one into his mouth while his other hand explored the other one, pinching and rolling my nipple between his fingers, causing me to let out a moan as I ground my hips down on him.

We were probably moving too far too fast, but I didn't care. Every relationship I'd ever had, I'd always waited and almost tried to plan for the right time.

In a swift motion, he lifted me up, and I found myself under him on the couch, his mouth now exploring my body. I reached down between us, running my hand over the impressive bulge in his pants, causing him to let out a moan. I pulled at his belt and quickly pulled at the button and zipper on his pants just enough I could slip my hand inside.

"Fuck." He hissed as I took him in my hand, stroking his length.

I watched him; he closed his eyes, his face peaceful as I continued running my hand over him. His breath quickened as I ran my thumb over the bead of pre-cum that had gathered on the head of his cock.

He took hold of my hand, his hand shaking, and pulled my hand away from him, stopping me. When he looked down at me, I could see that his eyes were full of want. He placed my hand above my head and then gripped the other one, pulling it to over my head, and held them both there while he undid my pants with his free hand. In a matter of seconds, he'd slipped his hands into my panties and let out a groan as his fingers slipped through my soaked centre.

"You're fucking soaked." He moaned.

I closed my eyes and let out a guttural groan as his fingers ran softly over my clit, gently circling for a few seconds before he stopped and pulled at my pants. I lifted, letting him pull them down off my hips to give him better access.

Pushing my panties to the side, his fingers danced lightly over my throbbing centre, before he slid one finger, then two deep inside of me, his thumb finding and concentrating on my clit.

I bit my bottom lip as I tried to pull my hands free from his grasp. I was going to come. It would only be a matter of seconds if he didn't stop. Only he didn't stop. Instead, he increased his efforts and met my lips, stifling my moans.

I could feel myself tightening around his fingers. He let go of my hands and removed his fingers, leaving me empty and throbbing. He sat down, relaxed back, and patted his lap as he took his cock in his hand and began stroking it slowly.

I watched him as I slid my pants off. I leaned over and grabbed my purse from the table, reaching in and pulling out a condom. His eyes met mine as I held it out for him to take. Without a word, he opened it and rolled it on himself, then took hold of my hand and guided me. I straddled his lap as he slid down a little, then he took hold of my hips and guided me as he lined himself up at my entrance.

I closed my eyes as I felt him enter me, letting out a moan as I took him all the way inside, filling me and stretching me in ways I'd never been before. Then, with his hands on my hips, he gently guided my motion.

Resting my one hand on his knee, I leaned back a bit as he leaned forward and sucked one of my nipples into his mouth. I reached down between us and with my free hand, running my fingers over my clit.

I could feel my orgasm building faster as he continued to guide my motion a little faster.

"You close?" he grunted.

I nodded, closing my eyes as he sucked my other nipple into his mouth, causing me to slip over the edge and tighten around him. His muscles tensed as he held onto me, stilling me as he poured himself inside of me.

Dalton

Two Weeks Later

"Something is different about you lately."

"What do you mean?" I questioned, glancing at Connie, the head RN of the hospital.

I glanced down at my watch to see I was running late to meet Amelia for lunch. We'd started having lunch together over at The Cooling Rack. Even though many doctors and nurses ate there, we'd found a booth in the back that was away from prying eyes. We'd only started doing this since we'd slept together a couple of weeks ago. Until that time, we'd eaten in the cafeteria separately. We'd promised each other that we'd keep work life separate from our personal life, but we wanted to spend our time together when we were off the clock, so this was the best way.

"I don't know, you seem....less cranky. Almost as if you've...dare I say it..."

"Connie...don't start that," I grumbled, not in the mood to put out rumors.

Connie was Eastport's gossip column. You wanted to know something about anyone, all you needed to do was ask her. She also had a tendency to make up whatever she wanted about people, which often led to some very nasty rumors being spread around. That was last thing I needed or wanted was rumors to be spread around about my new relationship with Amelia, true or not.

"I've noticed you haven't been eating in the cafeteria..." she continued, as if I hadn't said a word.

"What are you, my keeper? I've been taking lunch at odd hours the past couple of weeks." I shrugged. "Patient load has been heavier than normal."

Connie gave me with curious look. It was a completely viable answer, and one that someone couldn't dispute.

"Is that okay with you?" I questioned, my tone taking on more of its usual sound. Connie said nothing. She turned her head and stared straight ahead. "That's what I thought," I murmured just as the elevator doors opened.

The moment she'd stepped out of the elevator, I hit the close button and pressed the button for the main floor.

AMELIA WAS SITTING in our usual spot when I arrived. She glanced up from the article she was reading in the paper and smiled.

"I didn't think you were coming."

"And miss lunch with you? Never," I said, sitting across from her. "Did you order?"

"Yep, I got you the burger. Is that okay?"

"Sounds great," I said, letting out a breath as I slid into the seat across from her.

She studied me with a curious look. "What's going on?"

"What?" I asked. "It's nothing. Don't worry about it."

"Don't tell me not to worry about it. You look angry."

I reached out and took her hand in mine. I didn't want to spend our time together talking about Connie and her questions. I wanted to spend it with Amelia, laughing and talking about our plans for the upcoming weekend.

"It's nothing. Don't worry about it. Now, I was thinking about this weekend, the family holiday party... what time should we pick you up?"

Amelia looked at me with worry in her eyes.

"You are planning on joining the kids and I, aren't you?"

She swallowed hard and gently shook her head no. "I don't think so, Dalton. I'm worried that people will talk if we arrive together."

"The kids will be crushed," I said, my voice low enough, so no one overheard.

She looked at me with concern. "Dalton, I gave it some thought. We promised not to mix work with our personal life. I feel that if we attend together, that is what we will be doing."

"Whoa, wait a minute. I know what we said, but the kids are looking forward to it. Claire was so excited when I told her you were joining us."

"I know, and to be honest, I probably should have given it more thought when you asked, instead of just agreeing to go. We both agreed to keep our situation under wraps at work."

I studied her. I could tell there was something she wasn't telling me. I suddenly wondered if perhaps Connie had questioned her as well yesterday when she'd picked up the extra shift in the emergency.

"We did, but there is nothing saying you didn't need a lift. Besides, what would be wrong with us inviting you to join us for the day? You do work for me, after all."

Amelia let out a sigh, but I could still see something was bothering her, but I didn't want to press her into telling me. I wanted her to talk to me when she was comfortable.

"I'll come by the house around four," she said, just as our lunch arrived.

I stood outside Santa's Workshop with Amelia, waiting for Claire and Tommy to visit Santa. We'd shared a wonderful afternoon together, laughing, doing crafts with the kids, and singing songs. I could tell both the kids loved Amelia. They'd started coming around more once they caught us kissing one night in the kitchen before dinner. That had taken some explaining, but thankfully, I'd handled it well.

I was afraid of their questions. There was no doubt about it. They'd never seen me with another woman; they'd barely seen me with their mother. However, I remained calm and answered them. It seemed easier when I followed my heart for the answers instead of my head.

"I'm going to use the washroom," Amelia whispered.

"No problem. I'm sure we will be here." I winked.

I wanted to lean over and kiss her before she left my side, but I stopped myself, remembering where we were.

I took pictures of both the kids when it was their turn to speak with Santa and waited while they were both given their special present from Santa himself. They both came running over to me with their wrapped gifts, begging me to open them.

"Well, I think we should wait for Amelia, don't you think?" I questioned, glancing down at my watch, wondering where she could be. She'd been gone for over a half hour. "Perhaps we will save them for home."

"I guess," Claire said.

"What about you, Tommy?" I questioned, looking around the room for a sign of her.

"Fine," he whined.

It was then I spotted Amelia. She came into the room, her eyes red, and immediately made her way over to us.

"What is it?" I questioned, concern filling me.

"Can we just go? Like right now," she said, turning and making her way toward the door.

I glanced down at Claire and Tommy and ushered them both to the coat check, where I grabbed all our jackets and the three of us made our way toward the car.

Amelia was silent the entire drive back to my place. Almost the minute we were inside, I sent the kids upstairs to get ready for dinner and turned to find Amelia still standing at the door, her coat still on.

"What are you doing?"

"I'm going to head home. I'm not feeling very well."

I studied her, knowing full well there was something wrong. I'd worked with her far too long and knew when she was sick. This wasn't sick, she was upset. Hell, I was normally the cause of her anger, so I knew the difference.

"Amelia, if this is going to work between us, we have to be honest with one another."

"Dalton, it's nothing, really."

She met my eyes. She was trying to be strong, but I could see the worry filling hers. Something had happened while she'd been in that bathroom. I studied her, almost not wanting to ask what I already knew.

"Did Connie…"

That was the only word she had to hear. She turned away from me to hide her eyes. Anger filled me. It was fine she'd tried getting to me, but I knew Amelia wouldn't be able to fight her. It wasn't in her nature.

"She confronted you?"

"I've got to go." She sniffled, and without another word, she took off out the front door.

Amelia

Three Weeks Before Christmas

No matter how many times Dalton had asked, I hadn't told him what it was Connie had said the night of the kids' Christmas party. In the last week, we'd gone to work separately, we'd had lunch separately, and I'd done nothing but pull away. It wasn't because I was confused about how I felt about him, because I wasn't. Dalton wasn't who he was at work. He was a kind man who was capable of love and passion. It was because of Connie and the hatred and threats she'd spewed at me. So, for me, pulling away was the answer.

I knew Dalton was confused. I could see it in his eyes every time he looked at me. I'd become cold and withdrawn and absolutely hated myself for it. It wasn't like me to be this way toward him, especially without telling him why. He'd even tried to get me alone for an explanation, but each time I had a reason why I couldn't talk.

That was, until last night.

Charlotte had left for the day, and I was busy in the copy room putting away supplies when he'd come in and shut the door behind him. He placed his hands on my hips and placed a gentle kiss on the side of my neck.

Instantly, I thought I was going to break at the feel of him behind me. It was then he confessed to missing me and wanted to know if I would come join him and the kids for the night. Another kiss to the side of the neck and I was his. I couldn't turn him down.

I looked up from the kids' Christmas list and saw Dalton come into the living room carrying a bottle of wine and two glasses. He stopped, turning down the lights, gave me that sexy smile, and sat down beside me.

"Care for a drink?"

I placed the list on the table and smiled. "I'd love one."

He opened the wine and began pouring the two glasses as he met my eyes.

"I'm glad you joined us tonight," he said, handing me my glass, then clinking his against mine.

"Same." I softly smiled as I took a sip.

"I've missed you."

I nodded. "Dalton, I've missed you as well, and I'm sorry I've been avoiding you."

I saw the questions in his eyes, but I also knew he knew it had to do with why I'd run.

"She can be awful," he said quietly, studying me. "She confronted me too, a couple of days before the party."

I looked up at him, shocked that he hadn't told me that night. Perhaps had I not run and talked with him, he would have told me. Although he too could have brought the fact that she confronted him to me as well, to warn me if nothing more.

"What did she say to you?" he questioned.

I took another sip of my wine and looked up at him. "She claimed she knew why you request my help in the ER when you aid down there."

Dalton frowned. "I request your help because you are a fucking exceptional nurse. No other reason."

I felt my cheeks heat at his admission. "I know. She was referring to a conversation we'd had before anything happened between us, but I know Connie. She is great at twisting situations and words around. The things she's made up..."

"You don't need to explain. I've heard," Dalton said, taking my hand in his. "You also need to stand up to her."

"I don't know. She's my boss." I shrugged, worried how this could turn out. "She is the head RN."

"Who could be viewed as harassing you. Especially if

she is making things up about your personal life, which in turn is affecting your work life."

I knew Dalton was right, but I also worried what would happen if she reported us to human resources. However, since we hadn't made our situation public, we could just deny it and it would go away. They may watch us for a while, but not forever.

"Just hold your ground, okay? She is your boss at the hospital, but also remember I am as well. Just remember that."

I nodded and welcomed his lips to mine.

THE NEXT MORNING, I walked through Eastport Mall trying to find a Christmas gift for Claire and Tommy. I'd picked a couple of ideas off their lists with Dalton's help, and since it was my day off, I figured today was a good day to find something.

I stood inside the toy store singing along to "Grandma Got Run Over by a Reindeer" when I heard someone call my name. I turned around to see Connie. Irritation filled me as she approached me with a smile. I swallowed hard as I smiled back.

"Hey, Connie," I said, doing my best to focus on finding exactly what action figure it was Tommy had asked for.

"So, what are you doing here?" she questioned.

I gave her a questioning look, wondering why she was so interested in why I was here, and she let out a little laugh. "What do you mean?" I asked.

"Well, what I mean is this is a toy store, and you don't have kids."

I took in a deep breath as I picked up a box I was certain was the correct toy and began looking it over. "Shopping for a friend," I bit out.

"You realize I'm not stupid. There is word floating around the hospital that has me a little concerned."

"Oh? What would that be?" I said, picking up another box and giving it a once-over, trying not to react to what she was saying.

"That you and Dalton are seeing one another?"

"Is that so?" I questioned, doing my best to keep my composure.

"Yes."

"Well, people have their lines crossed because we are nothing more than friends, Connie," I said, putting the box back on the shelf, continuing to look at the other ones.

"You realize I see how you two look at one another?"

I picked up the next box. "How would that be?"

"Don't pretend you don't know. Plus, I've never seen Dalton recommend anyone, yet he has recommended you time and time again."

"Perhaps it's because he thinks I'm good at my job. Did that thought cross your mind?"

Connie studied me, saying nothing, but wore this small smirk.

"What?" I questioned.

"That's it isn't it. I'm correct. You're seeing him."

"No."

"Yes, you are. You don't lie well. Plus, if you knew he thought you were good at your job, it wouldn't have shocked you the day I told you about him recommending you. You yourself know what he is like to work for. Which leads me to believe that is why he was recommending you to begin with. Because the two of you are together."

I shook my head. I could feel my cheeks heating, and I knew there was no way I could play into this anymore. She'd be able to tell from my expression that what she was saying was true.

"That's it, isn't it? You two are together." A funny look washed over her face as she stood up a little straighter. It was enough to frighten me. "Amelia, you realize that it's against hospital policy to date a superior, don't you?"

"For the hundredth time, we aren't dating. We are friends," I gritted, my irritation growing bigger by the second.

Connie studied me, and I almost thought she believed me until she gave me an evil smile and shook her head.

"You know, Amelia, I've always liked you, and I'd love

to believe you, but one girl mentioned to me a couple of days ago that she saw the two of you at The Cooling Rack together, eating lunch."

"So what?" I said, shoving the list into my back pocket. "We were two colleagues having lunch. What's wrong with that?"

"Nothing, if it were true. However, I've never known someone who hates someone to have lunch with said person, or to help them with his kids, or to hold hands."

I went to walk away, tired of listening to this craziness. She was trying to get me to crack, and I couldn't allow her to know how close I was to doing so.

"I'll be talking to the proper channels later this week at work," she called out.

"Do whatever you feel you need to do, Connie," I said as I turned and made my way toward the exit, worry filling me.

I rushed to my car and then sped out of the parking lot back to Dalton's, ready to tell him everything, but when I got inside, he was on the phone and it looked serious.

I poured myself a hot coffee and sat down, fretting about the news I had to tell him. I listened as he spoke; it sounded like it was about a patient. Finally, he said he'd be there soon and then hung up the phone.

Dalton

IT WAS nice of her to leave one light on when I'd returned from the hospital. I'd felt awful about having to leave her with the kids when I'd gotten the call. One of my patients was being admitted into the hospital and had insisted on speaking with me. When I'd told her about the call, she'd insisted she agreed with me that I should go.

I'd offered to call Mrs. Jenkins to come stay with the kids, but Amelia absolutely refused and said she'd stay and get their dinner. I'd messaged her an hour ago just as I was wrapping up and she'd told me they had all gone to bed with no problems, to take as long as I needed. I'd expected her to be up when I arrived, but the house was dark and quiet—all but the one light.

I slipped my shoes off and shut the light off, heading upstairs to my bedroom. I could see light spilling into the hallway from under the bedroom door and quietly opened the door, expecting to find Amelia awake, but she was on her back, dressed in one of my T-shirts, sound asleep, with a book open, resting across her chest.

I softly smiled and went around to her side of the bed, gently taking the book from her chest, careful not to wake her. I'd just bookmarked her spot and shut the light off when she let out a soft moan and opened her eyes, looking up at me with hazy eyes.

"Dalton? What...what time is it?"

"It's late," I whispered. "Go back to sleep. I'll just be a minute." I cupped her cheek and placed a kiss on her forehead.

When I returned, she'd slipped under the covers and was lying on her side. I crawled in under the covers and wrapped my arms around her, pulling her back against me.

"How did it go?" she asked quietly.

"Okay," I whispered, pressing a kiss to her cheek.

I wasn't sure I wanted to discuss what had happened at the hospital tonight. It had been so long since I'd had a close interaction with a patient who was dying; I wasn't sure I knew how to deal with it anymore.

She rolled over, facing me, studying my eyes in the dimly lit room, then without a word pressed a kiss to my lips.

"I know it was hard for you to go, but I'm glad you went."

"Me too."

I pulled her into me, holding her tight. I needed to feel her close to me right now. I needed to know she was here.

"Tommy and Claire were talking to me about getting a tree tonight."

I couldn't help but chuckle. "Is that so?"

"They wondered if I would join you guys on that venture."

I looked down at her moonlit face, waiting to hear her answer. We'd barely been seeing one another a month, but to me it felt as if we had been together for much longer, and I already knew I was falling for her. Hell, if I were honest with myself the day she walked into my office for her interview, I'd thought about what it would be like to have a relationship with her. That had scared me so bad I could do nothing but be an ass to her, but she'd finally broken down my barriers.

"What did you tell them?"

"Nothing. I wasn't sure how you'd feel about me tagging along for that family time."

I frowned. "You weren't sure?"

She looked up at me, those large brown eyes staring back at me, and shook her head.

"I'd love to have you with us." I winked. "If you want to be, that is."

"I'd love to join you."

I pushed myself up onto my forearm and looked into her eyes. Placing my hand on her cheek, I lowered myself and placed a kiss on her lips, my tongue washing through her mouth. She wrapped her arms around me, and as I deepened the kiss, she let out a tiny moan.

***

"HERE'S a hot chocolate for you, and one for you, Tommy, and one for you," I said, handing Amelia her cup.

"Extra marshmallows?" she countered.

I smiled and winked. "You know it. Now, let's venture off and find a tree, shall we?"

"Yes!" Tommy shouted, slipping his gloved hand into Amelia's as Claire shoved hers into Tommy's.

I smiled at Amelia as the four of us walked through the gates of the second largest tree lot in Eastport. Christmas had always been a hard time ever since Kenzie died. The kids and I had done our best, but the three of us had struggled through the holidays. I knew my attitude hadn't helped things, but this year with Amelia in my life, I felt lighter than I had in a long time.

As we walked around, she started singing Christmas carols, which got the kids going, and soon the four of us were all singing "Jingle Bells" as we walked around the lot together. Finally, Claire pointed at a tree, claiming it was the perfect one, which, upon closer inspection, we all agreed.

"Is this the tree?" the attendant at the tree lot asked.

I looked down at both kids, who both stared up at me with goofy smiles. I couldn't help but chuckle and nod.

"Sure is. Can you wrap it for us? I'll go get the vehicle and pull it up to the gate over there," I said, pointing at the loading area.

"Sure can," he said, grabbing the tree and taking it over to the wrapping station.

I was just about to leave when Claire grabbed my hand.

"Dad, don't you think we should take a picture?"

Pictures were something we used to do when Kenzie was alive. The kids hadn't asked since she'd passed. However, I normally stopped at a grocery store lot and picked a tree from whatever was leftover two days before Christmas, and it was out by boxing day. I realized now I'd missed out on capturing memories that used to be important for the past few years.

I looked at Amelia and handed her my phone. "Would you?"

"Oh, sure." She smiled, pulling her glove off as she set her hot chocolate down on the ground.

"No, Dad. Amelia needs to be in the picture, too," Claire cried.

Dalton looked at me and smiled, then pulled his

phone from my hand, stopping a couple who were walking by and asking them if they would mind taking the picture. They took his phone and waited for us to get into position.

I wrapped my arm around Amelia, while Tommy and Claire moved in front of us. The four of us smiled as the couple took our picture, then Claire whispered something to Tommy, which made him laugh.

"What's so funny?" Amelia questioned.

Tommy looked up at the two of us and grinned. "Claire says you two should kiss in the next picture," he said, covering his mouth as he giggled.

I couldn't help but smile and asked the couple if they'd mind taking a couple more pictures, which both of them smiled and shook their heads.

I grabbed hold of Amelia and brought my lips to hers as Tommy looked up at us with wide eyes. It was then the couple snapped the picture.

"Thanks," I said and wished them both a Merry Christmas, only to turn back to see Amelia standing there with a worried look on her face.

I frowned as I made my way back over to them.

"What's wrong?" I whispered so only she could hear.

She looked up at me, her skin a little pale, and shook her head. "Nothing, I think we should just get the car," she said, giving me a weak smile.

I'D ASKED Amelia many times after we'd gotten home what was bothering her, only she refused to tell me, quickly changing the subject or focusing on the kids. She was going to head home after they'd gone to bed, but I convinced her otherwise, and she'd spent the night with me.

I'd just poured a cup of batter into the waffle maker when Amelia came into the kitchen.

"Morning," I said, as she helped herself to a cup of coffee.

"Morning." She softly smiled, only it barely reached her eyes.

She went to walk by me, but I stopped her, leaning in for a kiss.

"You ready to talk yet?" I whispered, not wanting the kids to think something was wrong.

She looked up at me with worried eyes and placed her hand on my chest. "I should have told you, but the day I was shopping, I ran into Connie. She was all over me, threatened…"

"What, that she was going to report us?" I questioned, looking at her.

She nodded.

"Did you do as I suggested and stand up to her?"

She nodded. "I did. I denied everything, but she was

there last night. She saw us take the photo. She saw us kiss," she whispered, fighting back tears.

As I thought about what to say, the phone rang. I grabbed the receiver and answered it. As I listened, my heart raced, and I hung up the phone without saying a word. I stood there for a moment, trying to gather my thoughts, when I finally felt Amelia's hand on my arm and turned to look at her.

"Dalton, what is it?"

"That was human resources. They've asked that I attend a disciplinary meeting today at three."

Amelia looked at me, tears in her eyes, and was about to say something when her cell phone rang. She looked at me, grabbed her phone, and listened intently, then hung up.

"Who was that?" I questioned.

"Same as you," she whispered, giving me a worried look.

***

"Just remain calm and follow my lead, okay?" I whispered into her ear as she climbed out of the car. I placed my hand on her lower back.

She looked up at me, concern in her eyes. "Dalton, do you really think it's a good idea that we show up together?"

"Just remain calm and follow my lead. We have done nothing wrong."

"I'm not sure they are going to see it that way. I'm your subordinate. They could constrew this as me trying to keep my job or something." She shrugged.

"Amelia, please. They can say what they want. We know what the truth is." I leaned forward and placed a kiss on her forehead.

"Do you enjoy having your head on a chopping block?" she questioned.

"My head isn't on a chopping block. Come on, let's go," I said, guiding her toward the door.

Once inside, we made our way to the administrative floor and toward the Human Resources office. I wasn't backing down, and I wasn't putting up with any shit at this first meeting.

I allowed Amelia to walk into the room first, and then I followed to see Connie sitting in a chair across from Rose, the head of human resources.

Irritation flooded me as Rose nodded toward the two empty chairs.

"What is this about?" I barked, opening my suit jacket and sitting down beside Amelia.

"Well, Dalton, Amelia, a formal complaint has been brought to my attention and what it contains is rather disturbing," Rose said, opening a folder on her desk.

"Care to enlighten me?" I questioned.

"It's been brought to my attention that you are currently involved in a relationship with Amelia, your nurse on staff."

I kept a straight face and waited for her to continue.

"That you have been caught engaging in sexual relations in many parts of the hospital?"

I saw Connie turn and look at the pair of us from the corner of my eye. I cleared my throat and stood up, causing Rose to stop speaking.

"I think this meeting is over for now. I'll be getting in touch with my advocate, and I'd recommend Amelia do the same thing."

Rose looked over toward Amelia, who at first didn't move, but then stood up and nodded.

"I'll be getting in touch with mine as well."

I didn't hesitate. I opened the door to the room and walked out. Once I heard the door close, I turned and saw Amelia coming up behind me.

"I'm glad you followed my lead. Those accusations are..."

"Ridiculous," she finished.

"Yes. Let's head on home and call our—"

She held her hand, which stopped me from continuing. She looked to the floor, then to the wall behind me, anywhere but directly at me.

"Amelia, it's going to be—"

"No, Dalton, it won't be okay. This is a disaster. To be

honest, I just want to be alone so, I think for tonight, and for the next little while, I'm just going to stay at my place instead."

I didn't know what to say to her. I didn't want her to be alone, to have to deal with these things on her own, but I knew it was probably for the best, so I let her go.

Amelia

IT HAD BEEN five days since the meeting with Rose. When I'd gone into work the next day, she met me outside of the elevators and told me I would no longer be working in Dalton's office. Instead, I was being moved to the emergency department until further notice. I wasn't allowed to go in and get any of my things from the office until after hours, and I was to have no contact with Dalton, either.

As I made my way past the office, I saw Connie wave at me from behind the desk. Irritation flooded me, followed by anger.

I made my way into the emergency department, thankful that today was the last day of my work week, and was immediately greeted by Sawyer.

"Hey, Amelia. Constance is here to see you. You can use my office."

I frowned, not having a clue who Constance was. Sawyer must have seen the look on my face because he stopped and gave me a small smile.

"Constance is your employee advocate."

"Thanks."

My stomach turned as I made my way toward Sawyer's office. I did not know what to expect, what sort of things had been said in that formal complaint because when I'd gotten my copy yesterday, I was too upset to read it. Instead, I'd drank down a bottle of wine and passed out after work.

I stopped outside of his door, my mind racing with all the things that I imagined Connie would have or could have said in that complaint.

I took a deep breath and then pushed the door open, stepping into the room to see a woman sitting behind Sawyer's desk making some notes. She looked up, lowered her glasses to the tip of her nose, and cleared her throat.

"Amelia White?"

"Yes," I said, swallowing hard, certain I probably looked as if I were going to be sick.

"I'm Constance Granger. I'm here to aid you through this hearing. Why don't you have a seat?" she said, standing up and pouring me a glass of water from the pitcher on the desk.

I slipped into the chair and placed my purse at my feet,

thankful to sit down as it helped the room to stop spinning.

"So, why don't you start by telling me about your relationship with Dalton?"

What did she want to know? Panic filled me now that I realized I probably should have read the complaint. Since I did not know what it even said, I did not know how to answer her question.

"What about my relationship?" I questioned.

"Oh, I guess I should be a little clearer. About your working relationship. How long have you been working with him?"

I nodded. "I've been working for him for a year."

"And how would you describe him as a boss?"

"I enjoy working for him."

She wrote my answer, then looked up at me. "Some of the staff around the hospital say he can be difficult to get along with. Would you say that is true?"

I shrugged. "Maybe at first, but once you get to know him and what he expects, it gets easier."

"Amelia, you have worked for many doctors in this hospital. Wouldn't you say that every doctor expects the same standard of work?"

"Of course."

"Do you not provide the same work ethic to them all?"

"Yes."

"Then what is it you mean by once you learn what he expects."

Alarm filled me. I'd clearly chosen the wrong words.

"In the report, it was mentioned that you often complained about Dalton to others. Then suddenly you stopped. It was shortly after he requested you specifically to come to the emergency department one day. After that, you helped with him and his daughter in the cafeteria. You were also seen holding hands and kissing in public places, not to mention being caught in the act. So exactly what does this man expect?"

I frowned. That was the day his daughter had the meltdown over her hair. That was the day I'd helped fix it for her in the change room.

I smiled, trying to hide my nerves. "Yes, the cafeteria. His daughter had somewhat of a hair catastrophe and was having a meltdown. I helped fix her hair for her."

"I see, and you were spotted with her shortly after that in the pharmacy on West Road," she said, looking back at the complaint.

I frowned. Had Connie been following me? "Well, yes, she was having a female emergency."

Constance looked up at me and stopped writing.

"I was simply helping her get some female hygiene products. Since her mother died, she felt better speaking with another woman. I'd told her it was fine to call me."

"Dalton is an OB/GYN, do you not think he could take care of that for his own daughter?" she questioned, looking me straight in the eye.

"Well, yes, but—"

"But what? What it looks like to me is that perhaps Dalton called you because he wanted to get closer to you, and the only way he could do that was to get you out of the office and perhaps into his own private space. Or maybe you were looking for a promotion that Connie wouldn't give you?"

"That is ridiculous."

"Is it? People tell me Dalton is hard to please, so it only makes sense that promotions wouldn't be handed out quickly. Also, word around the hospital is that he works long hours, leaving his children at home with nannies, so he doesn't need to deal with them. It was also reported that you were Christmas shopping in a toy store, yet you have no children of your own. After being confronted and denying the allegations, someone saw you out with the entire family looking for a Christmas tree, where it was reported the two of you kissed for a photo, which apparently, when you noticed, there was a look of discomfort on your face."

The room spun out of control. The look of discomfort had been because I'd seen Connie watching us. There had been no other reason.

"Also—"

I cut her off. I didn't like what she was suggesting, nor that she was siding with the complaint. She was supposed to be here to hear my side of the story and look at the entire thing objectively, not have a preformed opinion.

"I'm sorry, but I need to use the washroom for a moment." Getting up and grabbing my purse, I left the room.

Once I was in the washroom, I locked the main door and went into one stall. I pulled my phone from my purse, panic filling me at her suggestion. I did not know what to do, and since I hadn't seen or talked to Dalton all week, we hadn't come up with a plan.

I was about to dial his office when I realized Connie would be the one answering the phones. She was probably already aware of the fact that Constance was here to see me as well. So, I dialed his personal cell phone, hoping and praying he wasn't in his own meeting or in with a client. Only it didn't ring. Instead, it went directly to his voicemail.

I covered my mouth, trying to stifle my cries as I listened to his message. Once I heard the beep, I sniffled and tried hard to regain composure, only I blubbered into the phone, no doubt not making any sense, then I hung up, wiped my eyes, and went to the sink. I splashed some cold water on my face, took a few deep breaths, and then headed back to the meeting.

I sat back down in my chair and waited for Constance to look up from her notes. When she did, I cleared my throat. I wasn't sure how she was going to react to my next statement, but it needed to be said.

"I don't like how you are twisting what I say around to make Dalton look bad. He has in no way influenced me or preyed upon me, if that is what you are trying to get me to admit. He also has never passed me up for a promotion, since I've never applied or expressed interest in any," I said, trying to stand my ground.

Constance removed her glasses, then sat back in her chair. I could see she was thinking before she said anything, and when she did, I felt all the air leave the room.

"Amelia, it would be in your best interest for you to get on board with the narrative, especially if you'd like to keep your job."

What was she talking about? Did she really just give me this ultimatum, to turn against Dalton and go with the story or lose my job? I crossed my arms in front of me, trying to work through everything.

"Tell you what. Here is my card, you think about it. Call me no later than Monday and let me know what path you are going to take."

She bundled up the folder she had in front of her and shoved it into her case and then left the room. I felt nauseous and like I could faint. There was no way I could work today.

I reached over and grabbed a pen and pad of paper from Sawyers' desk and quickly scribbled a note, then gathered my things and slipped out the back door.

Dalton

I LISTENED to her muffled message and sobbing cries once I'd gotten into my car, trying to make out what she was saying. It was so garbled, I had to replay it.

As I listened carefully to the message, my heart raced. She mentioned something about being forced to follow along or be fired. When I got to the next message, it was her again, only the second message there was no way I could understand. It sounded as if she'd been outside when she'd called and left the message.

I gripped the steering wheel of the car, debating what to do. I'd been forewarned by my advocate not to have contact with her, but she was hurting and needed me. I hated the position Connie had put us in.

Almost as if on cue, Connie appeared, walking in front of my car on the way to hers. She held up her hand

and waved as if we were best friends, then signalled for me to roll my window down.

I hit the button, the cold winter air hitting my cheeks.

"Have a great night, Dalton. I am glad everything went well today with all the patients, and I look forward to getting more hands-on tomorrow!" she yelled as she waved.

Irritation flooded me. She was a horrible nurse, horrible with the patients, paperwork and reports hadn't been filed all week, I couldn't find anything I needed, and she was lazy as hell. The moment the office closed, she was out of there. How the hell she'd ever become the head RN baffled me. I now remembered why I'd denied her promotion when we worked together at the last hospital I was at.

My phone rang just as I started the engine. I grabbed it immediately, seeing it was Amelia. Only when I answered, the line went dead.

That was it. I didn't care that I'd been warned; I was going to her. This was absolutely ridiculous and beyond anything I could ever imagine could have happened because of this.

I knocked on the door of her apartment, waiting in the hall. I heard nothing as I listened at the door. Perhaps she wasn't home, I thought to myself. I was just about to turn and leave when I heard the door unlock. I stopped, turning in time to see her red, swollen eyes.

I pushed the door open and stepped inside, shutting it

behind me before I grabbed her and wrapped her in my arms. Almost immediately, she cried heavy sobs as I held her in my arms.

When she finally stopped and I let her go, she looked up at me.

"You shouldn't be here."

"I know, but when I got your message, I had to come. This is all my fault."

"What? No, it's not," she cried, getting upset again. "I just want this all to go away. It was so horrible today." She sniffled.

I'd never seen her this upset, not even when I'd had my worst days, so I could only imagine how bad it must have been.

"It will soon, and it is my fault. I was the one who pursued you. This is all on me."

"What are you saying?"

I'd battled internally all day with my thoughts on how to deal with the situation. This was Amelia's livelihood, and I knew if they gave her any type of ultimatum, which, from what I'd made out in her message, they had, that they meant what they said. She'd be without a job before Christmas if she didn't side with them. Even though this was my livelihood as well, I was in a far better position to give it all up.

"What I'm saying is that I've given things a lot of thought and—"

"I'm not siding with them, Dalton, I'm not. They are accusing you of things that never happened. I refuse to allow them to do that to you."

I placed my hands on her shoulders and met her eyes. "You don't need to side with them because there is nothing to side with. I'm just going to come clean."

"About what? What they are accusing you of? That isn't fair, and I won't let you do that," she said, crossing her arms in front of her, that stubborn, fiery side of her that I loved so much coming out.

"Look, I know how much you love this job. It's your passion. What you need to do is put a little trust in me and not worry about how things turn out for me. I will not be angry at the outcome. It will be what it is. It will change nothing between us."

"I'm not siding with them. I'm not accusing you of something so heinous. You did nothing. All they did was twist my words to fit the story they want to hear. It's wrong. I don't understand how you can tell me to do what they want."

"Whoa, I just said you don't need to side with them. You need to put your trust in me and what I'm about to do."

She got quiet as she looked at me. I could tell she wanted to say something, so I waited.

"What are you going to do?" she finally questioned, her voice shaking.

I couldn't help but softly smile at her. If it meant that everything would go away, I'd do this over again if ever it came up again.

"I need you to put your trust in me. I'm going to protect you in any way I have to," I said, swallowing hard.

"What? What are you talking about?"

"I'm going to do whatever it takes to protect you because when you love someone, that is what you do."

It was the first time I'd said it, and even though we hadn't been dating all that long—less than six weeks I'd fallen head over heels for her—truth was, I'd fallen for her a long time ago, way before we'd ever even become friends. I'd only realized it today, as I looked around my office, at the mess before me, waiting and wanting to hear that playful giggle she always gave when she was working so hard at annoying me with the say please and thank you speech.

Tears filled her eyes as I looked at her and she brought her hands to her eyes to clear them away.

"I'm in love with you, and that is what I am going to tell them," I said, bringing my lips to hers.

When I broke our kiss, not another word was said. I slipped from her apartment and took off down the hall, leaving her until the hearing.

Amelia

Christmas Eve

I STOOD in front of the disciplinary committee, my hands together as I waited while Connie gave her update to them. How the hell they even allowed that was beyond me. The woman was going to go to hell if karma truly was a bitch, I thought to myself.

Since I hadn't liked Constance or her ultimatum, I faced the board on my own, and to be honest, ignoring all that had been said once I'd finally read the complaint. I planned to file my complaint against her with Dalton's help once this was all over.

I took a deep breath as I watched Connie speak with

the members of the committee. Each time she said something, she glanced at me over her shoulder, giving me some form of a smile. I could only imagine what she was telling them.

When she finished making up more lies, she made her way to the chair she'd been sitting in and took a seat, waiting while they made some notes and then turned their attention to me.

"Amelia, would you care to say anything before we begin?" one of the board members questioned.

I nodded. "I came to work for Dalton Frost a year ago. While to begin with, he was difficult to work with, we soon fell into a routine that worked. Over the course of the year, I got to know him and started helping with his family when his daughter had a hair emergency for a school dance. I found out that Dalton was a widow, and being a girl who'd lost a parent at a young age, I took to his daughter Claire quickly and told her if she needed anything she could always ask me.

"Soon after that, she'd called with a bit of an emergency that only a girl would be comfortable sharing with her mother. While I knew she didn't have a mother, I figured I'd help her out. Over time, spending time with Dalton and his family, things developed slowly into more. Neither of us planned for that to happen, but I fell in love with him, and while I'm not proud of the fact that it was being broadcast to my fellow employees the way it has," I said, glancing over to Connie, "I'm not sorry that it happened. You all yourself know you can't help who you fall in love with."

Connie rolled her eyes at me as I let out the breath I was holding. The board members then turned toward Dalton.

"Dalton, anything you'd like to add?"

Dalton stood up and smiled at me. Then cleared his throat. "All Amelia said is true. There was never any intent behind her helping me with my children. The claims of the situation are false. We have never, nor would we ever, have any sexual relations during working hours. That was something the pair of us laid out immediately when we started dating. However, the truth is I fell in love with her, and I will accept whatever comes my way from all of this because she is more than worth it."

He reached over and took my hand in his, softly smiling at me, not caring what the board members thought.

It was then I heard Connie mumble, "Oh boy."

When I turned to look her way, she was rolling her eyes as she crossed her arms in front of her chest. The board members even glanced at her as they spoke amongst themselves before looking to us.

"If you'd like to take a bit of a break while we discuss our decision, you may. We will continue in ten minutes."

Dalton placed his hand on the small of my back and

guided me to the door. Once outside in the hall, he pulled me in for a hug and whispered in my ear that he was proud of me. We both watched as Connie moved down the hall and took a seat far away from us.

Almost twenty minutes later, Rose stepped out of the room and nodded toward us. We both went back in and took our seats. As Connie approached the door, Rose shut it to shield whatever it was she was saying to her and then came in without her. I couldn't help but look to Dalton with curiosity as to why she wasn't allowed to return, but the look I got from him told me to calm down a bit until we heard the end.

Rose sat down and then looked at us both. She softly smiled and held out a copy of the employee handbook.

"First, I'd like to start by saying that the committee and I have decided the there was no wrongdoing here at all. You both have been given a copy of this handbook, and I know you have both read it."

"We have," Dalton and I said in unison.

"So while there is nothing wrong with dating co-workers here at Eastport, we have a clause that states that there will be no relations allowed between boss and employee. Now, we have gone over everything, and since Amelia, yes, works in your clinic, you are not her direct boss. The head RN is, which is Connie."

I glanced over to Dalton. The clouds finally seemed to lift.

"Now, we don't see any issue with what has transpired between the pair of you. What we have an issue with is this complaint and the fact that it seems Connie has been harassing Amelia. Everything in this complaint leads me to believe that she maybe has even been following you around, looking for things."

I couldn't believe my ears. Dalton was right, he'd said it first, that the board may see this as just that. I looked over at him, but he kept his eyes forward.

"So, we plan to investigate that after the holidays. So, your new boss, Amelia, will be assigned to you next week until we do this investigation. Now, we need you both to fill out this paperwork, just so we have it on record that you are involved, but we see no reason you both cannot continue to work together in any capacity."

Dalton stood up, taking my hand in his. I too stood, and we both thanked the entire committee before leaving the room.

We were partway down the hall when Connie came walking toward us, sneering at us both as she passed. I couldn't help but turn around and watch as Rose waited for her at the door, which was closed once Connie stepped into the room.

I turned to Dalton, relief flooding me as our eyes met. It was over; we weren't in the wrong, and it looked as if my Christmas wish had come true. Karma had shown its face.

"What do you say we head over to the store, grab some

wine and some dinner, and head home to the kids?" Dalton questioned.

"I'd love that," I whispered as his lips met mine.

Amelia

Christmas Night - 1 year Later

The kids were already in bed.

I sat in the living room, admiring the ring on my hand. After the hearing last year, things moved rather fast for us. I ended up moving in with Dalton and the kids at the beginning of summer and never looked back.

"Think you can tear your eyes away enough to have some wine?" Dalton questioned, holding the glass out in front of me.

I let out a tiny giggle, taking the glass from him.

"Sorry, it's just so beautiful," I said, looking back down at my hand.

"I know. Looks even better on you." He winked.

He placed his arm on the back of the couch, and I shifted so I could lean into him. The moment I rested against him, he placed his arm around me and kissed the top of my head.

"You happy?" he questioned.

"Am I happy? You aren't seriously asking me that, are you?" I asked, taking a sip of my wine.

"I am. I just want to make sure."

"I am," I assured him. "I can't wait to plan our wedding."

"Same here, and I think the first person we should add to the guest list is Connie."

I couldn't help but laugh at his suggestion.

"I'll get right on that."

Connie had been fired from Eastport at the beginning of the year. Apparently, when she lodged another complaint against Dalton at the beginning of this year, they had her followed and found that she had been following both of us. Turns out she was seeking Dalton's approval since she'd never gotten over the fact I'd passed her over for promotions time and time again. When I confronted her on the second complaint she finally broke down and told human resources that. It didn't matter that she held a high position at Eastport, she hated Dalton with a passion and wanted to win his approval.

"You know what I think?" he whispered in my ear as music quietly played.

"What?"

"I think I'd like to see you in nothing but that ring," he said, pressing a kiss to the side of my neck.

"Is that so?" I questioned, swallowing hard as a wave of excitement rolled through my body.

"Right there, in front of the fireplace," he whispered.

My mind shot back to the first time we'd been together, right here on this couch. How I'd known he was for me and I was for him. We'd fit so well together.

He stood up, placed his glass on the table in front of us, and then turned, taking my glass from my hand. He then took hold of my hand, grabbing the blanket that lay on the back of the couch. Walking around the table, he spread the blanket out on the floor then wiggled his forefinger at me, in a come-to-me motion.

I shyly smiled as I always did and got up to go to him. He pulled me in his arms and kissed me deeply. This was how I wanted us to be forever—in love, with no one in our way.

At first, I thought the name Frost was so fitting, but I'd been wrong. He had a wonderful, caring heart, and he was warm and passionate, and I had never been so happy to be the owner of his frost-less heart.

Doctors of Eastport General Series

I hope you enjoyed my book, Doctor Frost, which is part of the shared world Doctors of Eastport General.

Would you like to read all of them? Find them here on Kindle Unlimited.

Come on in and meet the new ER Physicians, Surgeons, Specialists, Residents, and patients that occupy the rooms and halls of the largest hospital on the coast of Rhode Island. You may even run into some of the doctors from Season 1. We hope you are ready to fall in love with all the new sexy stories that take place inside the walls of Eastport General Hospital.

Season 3

Doctor Grinch by Amy Stephens
Doctor Clause by CA King
Doctor Charmer by Mel Walker
Doctor Jingle Bells by TL Mayhew
Doctor Do-Over by EM Shue
Doctor Frost by S.L. Sterling
Doctor Holliday by Tracy Broemmer

Season 2

Doctor Irresistible – Syd Ryan
Doctor Mistake – Amy Stephens
Doctor Divine – Tracy Broemmer
Doctor, Please – Celeste Granger
Doctor Frank Enstein – CA King
Doctor Change of Heart – Amber Ghe
Doctor Rescue – Mel Walker
Doctor Delectable – TL Mayhew
Doctor Love – Adryan Hart
Doctor Danger – Pandora Snow
Doctor Stuck-Up – A.N. Waugh
Doctor Sinful – E.M. Shue
Doctor Right – S.L. Sterling

Season 1

Doctor Mistake by Amy Stepns

Doctor Feelgood by Amy Stephens
Doctor D's Orderly Affair by CA King
Doctor Trouble by E.M. Shue
Doctor Temptation by Syd Ryan
Dueling Doctors by DC Renee
Doctor Sexy by TL Mayhew
Doctor Fix-It by Mel Walker
Doctor One of a Kind by Anjelica Grace
Doctor Casanova by Emma Nichole
Dirty Doctor by Amanda Richardson
Doctor All Nighter by Adora Crooks
Doctor Desire by S.L. Sterling

GET A FREE BOOK

Sign up for my newsletter and I'll send you a free book.

https://geni.us/NLSignupBackMatter

What is coming next from S.L. Sterling

Under the Mistletoe Spice and Seduction
December 2024
https://geni.us/UndertheMistletoe

Returning to Me (Willow Valley)
December 2024
https://geni.us/ReturningtoMeWV6

ACE (Vegas MMA)
January 2025
https://geni.us/AceVegasMMA

Two Minutes for Holding (Vancouver Dominators)
Coming in 2025
https://geni.us/TwoMinutesforHolding

Follow S.L. Sterling

Did you know that bookbub has a feature where you can follow me and it will send you an alert when I release a book or put a title on sale? Sign up here and make sure you stay in the loop.

Bookbub:
https://geni.us/SLSterlingBookbub

Website
https://www.authorslsterling.com

Facebook
https://geni.us/SLSterlingFB

Twitter
https://geni.us/SLSterlingTwitter

Instagram
https://geni.us/SLSterlingInstagram

Tiktok
https://geni.us/slsterlingtiktok

Reader Group

https://geni.us/SapphiresReaderGroup

Goodreads
https://geni.us/SterlingGoodreads

Newsletter
https://geni.us/NLSignupBackMatter

About the Author

USA Today Bestselling Author S.L. Sterling was born and raised in southern Ontario. She now lives in Northern Ontario Canada and is married to her best friend and soul mate and their two dogs.

An avid reader all her life, S.L. Sterling dreamt of becoming an author. She decided to give writing a try after one of her favorite authors launched a course on how to write your novel. This course gave her the push she needed to put pen to paper and her debut novel "It Was Always You" was born.

When S.L. Sterling isn't writing or plotting her next novel she can be found curled up with a cup of coffee, blanket and the newest romance novel from one of her favorite authors.

In her spare time, she enjoys camping, hiking, sunny destinations, spending quality time with family and friends and of course reading.

To be notified of new releases or sales, join S.L. Sterling's private Mailing List.
https://geni.us/NLSignupBackMatter

Get even more of the inside scoop when you join S.L. Sterling's private Facebook group, Sterling's Silver Sapphires: https://geni.us/SapphiresReaderGroup

Other Books by S.L. Sterling

Standalone

It Was Always You

On A Silent Night

Bad Company

Back to You this Christmas

Fireside Love

Holiday Wishes

Saviour Boy

The Boy Under the Gazebo

The Greatest Gift

Into the Sunset

Letting You Go

The Spencer Brooks Diaries

Our Little Secret

Our Little Surprise

Our Little Wedding

The Malone Brother Series

A Kiss Beneath the Stars

In Your Arms

His to Hold

Finding Forever with You

Vegas MMA

Dagger

Doctors of Eastport

Doctor Desire

Doctor Right

Doctor Frost

All I Want for Christmas (Contemporary Romance Holiday Collection)

Willow Valley Series

Memories of the Past

To Trust my Heart

Letters from the Heart

What Once was Broken

Scars on my Heart

The Happy Holidates Series

Pop Tarts and Mistletoe

Champagne and Fireworks

Summer Nights and Fireflies

Vancouver Dominators

Inside the Penalty Box

Ten Minute Misconduct